D0000815

Pursued

Patricia H. Rushford

Jennie McGrady
Mystery Series

Pursued

Patricia H. Rushford

BETHANY HOUSE PUBLISHERS
MINNEAPOLIS, MINNESOTA 55438

PURSUED
Patricia Rushford

Cover illustration by Andrea Jorgenson

Coke is a registered trademark of the Coca-Cola Corporation.
Jacuzzi is a registered trademark of
Jacuzzi Brothers, Jacuzzi Inc.

Library of Congress Catalog Card Number 94–74536

ISBN 1–55661–333–4

Published by Bethany House Publishers
A Ministry of Bethany Fellowship, Inc.
11300 Hampshire Avenue South,
Minneapolis, Minnesota 55438

Printed in the United States of America

Dedicated to

Olga Bond
1912–1993

In loving memory
of my eighty-one-year-old aunt
who would have loved Jennie.

PATRICIA RUSHFORD is an award-winning writer, speaker, and teacher who has published almost twenty books and numerous articles, including *What Kids Need Most in a Mom* and her first young adult novel, *Kristen's Choice*. She is a registered nurse and has a master's degree in counseling from Western Evangelical Seminary. She and her husband, Ron, live in Washington state and have two grown children, six grandchildren, and lots of nephews and nieces.

Pat has been reading mysteries for as long as she can remember and is delighted to be writing a series of her own. She is a member of Mystery Writers of America, Society of Children's Book Writers and Illustrators, and Director of the summer conference Oregon Association of Christian Writers.

1

"You will help Allison, won't you, Jen?" Lisa capped her emerald polish and blew on her nails.

Uneasiness slithered through Jennie like a herd of lizards. The more adventurous part of her wanted to say, *Sure, I'll help. We'll have the creep who's been bugging Allison in jail before your nails are dry.* The other part . . . the one housing her intuition and what Mom would term good sense, argued, *Danger! No way! Stay out of it!*

Jennie sighed and decided to settle somewhere in the middle—at least for now. "I don't know," she finally answered as she unfolded her long legs and pushed away from the window seat. Then, tossing off the inner warnings, teased, "Does she use green fingernail polish?"

Lisa gave her cousin and best friend a scathing look. "What, you don't like my nails? I think they're great. They're a perfect match for my new green swimsuit. Brad will flip."

Jennie couldn't imagine Lisa's boyfriend flipping over anything—except maybe football. "He'll notice you—that's for sure. So will everyone else at the party. You'll look like a leftover leprechaun from the St. Patrick's Day Parade." Jennie grabbed a brush from her dresser and flopped on the bed next to Lisa. The "party" was Allison

7

Beaumont's big spring bash, to which practically everyone in town was invited, and to which Jennie had no intention of going.

"You're just jealous because you can't get your nails this long." Lisa bounced off the bed, keeping her hands stretched out in front of her.

"Yeah, well, considering what my nails—not to mention my body—has been through in the last month, it's no wonder." Just a week before, Jennie had narrowly escaped drowning, a fire, and a guy with murder on his mind.

Jennie pulled the brush through her long dark hair and took a deep breath. She was still having nightmares about him. Which was another reason she didn't particularly want to get involved with Allison. Of course the most important reason was that she wanted to be ready to start looking for Dad as soon as Gram came home. During Jennie and Gram's trip to Florida, Jennie had talked Gram into helping her find Dad. Now everything was on hold while Gram took care of some official business in Europe. J.B., Gram's FBI friend, had tried to sweep her away the minute their plane landed. "An important assignment" was all he'd said.

"Sorry," Gram told him. "Family comes first and I promised Jennie we'd work on finding Jason."

In the end, Jennie urged Gram to go. Working for the government meant making sacrifices—that much she'd learned when Dad had been alive. *No, scratch that, McGrady. He is still alive—just missing.*

Gram had only been gone for three days, and Jennie wished she could take it all back. Even if tracking down Allison's "secret admirer" did sound intriguing, the only case Jennie McGrady cared about at the moment was finding her father and bringing him home.

"I know you've been through a lot lately," Lisa said, interrupting Jennie's thoughts, "but Allison needs our help."

"Why doesn't she go to the police?"

"She has. The police haven't been able to come up with anything."

"Then how do you expect me to?" Jennie asked. "Just because I helped solve a couple of mysteries doesn't mean I'm about to hang a shingle on my door and call myself a private eye. Speaking of which, why don't her parents hire one? It's not like they can't afford to."

"Her parents agree with the police, that it's probably a prank. Allison says they keep telling her not to worry. Anyway, with all the scary stuff that's been in the news lately, she's afraid someone might be stalking her. She's really upset and I . . . ah . . . well, I sort of hinted that you might be willing to help."

"Lisa—"

"What if I help you?" Lisa interrupted. "We could spend a lot of time with her, maybe bug her phone and stake out her house . . . you know, do a surveillance kind of thing."

Trying to ignore the pleading look in Lisa's sea green eyes, Jennie scooted to the edge of the bed and lowered her head, letting her dark hair cascade over the side, then started brushing again. "Spending time with Allison is not my idea of a good time. Besides, it could be dangerous. From what you've told me the guy sounds like a real creep."

Lisa plopped back on the bed, careful to keep her fingers splayed out in front of her. "I know it could be scary, Jen, but think about Allison. She's about to go crazy. This guy's been after her ever since she got named Rose Princess. The worst thing so far was pulling the distributor caps out of their cars so she'd be late for the Rose Festival Parade."

The Rose Festival brought tourists from all over the world. Events began with each school choosing a princess. Then about the first week of June one of those princesses became the Rose Festival Queen.

"That's another possibility," Jennie offered as she flipped her hair back. "What if one of the girls who lost to Allison is jealous and is doing this to get back at her?"

Lisa frowned as she tested her nails for dryness. "Well, there was that thing with Paige Matthews. Remember?"

Jennie shook her head.

"Paige and Ed Brodie were going together, then over Christmas, when Paige went with her parents on vacation, Ed and Allison started going out. When Paige came home she was furious."

"I thought Paige and Allison were best friends."

"They are, now. After a couple of months Allison broke up with Ed, and a few weeks later he and Paige got back together. It was all a big misunderstanding."

"What about the other girls?"

Lisa thought a moment then said, "Na. We were all disappointed, but I think we're all happy for Allison. We're not sore losers." Lisa stopped for a second and tipped her head to the side. "Besides, this is definitely a guy."

"What makes you think so?"

"It started out being kind of romantic. He sent her a card and some flowers and signed it *Your Secret Admirer*. At first she thought it might have been some guy from school who has a crush on her."

"It might be." Jennie gathered her hair into strands and began braiding. "Or it might be a girl who wants Allison to think it's a guy."

Lisa wrinkled her nose at Jennie's suggestion. "The only guy I can think of right now is Jerry."

"Jerry Shepherd?" Jennie asked. "Jerry likes Allison?" The news disappointed her. She'd always thought of Jerry as intelligent and level-headed—not the sort who'd fall for a prima donna like Allison.

"He asked me a few weeks ago if I thought Allison would ever go out with him."

"What did you tell him?"

"That she might."

"How could you mislead Jerry like that! He's a nice guy. You should have told him he had about as much chance of dating Allison as he does Madonna."

Lisa ignored the sarcastic remark and sighed. "Love conquers all things."

"Only in the movies," Jennie mumbled. The only thing love had done for her lately was to make her miserable. Thoughts of Ryan tumbled into her head. They could have had so much fun this summer—romantic walks on the beach, holding hands, kissing. Only none of that was going to happen. Ryan had gone fishing in Alaska. And she was stuck in Portland.

"Anyway," Lisa was saying when Jennie tuned back in, "we both know Jerry wouldn't dream of hurting anyone. Got any other ideas?"

Jennie pushed her musings about love and Ryan aside and concentrated instead on who might have reason to get even with Allison. "Maybe somebody's playing practical jokes on her. You know, getting back at her for not inviting them to her parties or something."

"Could be, but I don't know of anyone that mean. Lately his notes have been getting more . . . I don't know . . . dangerous. The last one said, *I'm watching you.*" Lisa grimaced. "And she's been getting these spooky phone calls—anyway, I feel sorry for her. I told her I'd talk to you. Why don't you at least listen to her side—get to know her? Then decide. Even if we can't catch the guy, at least we can be there for her."

"Well . . . I guess I could talk to her." Jennie reached for a hair band and twisted it around the braid's end, then flipped it back over her shoulder.

"Great. I knew you'd do it." Lisa glanced at her watch. "She should be here any minute."

"What? Allison Beaumont is coming here . . . to my house?" Jennie grabbed the back of Lisa's neck and squeezed. "Lisa, it's almost nine-thirty!"

"Ah . . . I invited her to stay overnight."

"You what? It would serve you right if I smudged all your nails."

"Don't you dare." Lisa giggled and ducked away. "Jennie," Lisa said, sobering, "Allison's a really sweet person when you get to know her."

"Yeah, right. Tell that to the long string of guys she's dumped. . . . Besides, Mom will have a fit." Mom and her boyfriend, Michael, had taken Jennie's five-year-old brother, Nick, to a movie. And Mom did not like surprises.

"I've taken care of that too. I called her this afternoon before I came over. So you see, it's all set."

Jennie shook her head. "Did you tell her why Allison was coming?"

"Of course not. I just said we had a friend who really

needed our help right now." Lisa tossed back her thick mass of copper-colored curls and smiled. "She does, you know, and I think you'll be glad you agreed to help."

"I didn't say I'd help. I just said I'd talk with her." Jennie slipped off the bed and walked to her closet. "I'm not getting dressed." She stood in front of the mirror assessing her baggy purple sweats.

"Will you relax! It's not like she's Princess Di or anything."

The doorbell rang. "That's her." Lisa headed for the door, then stopped and turned around. "Aren't you coming?"

Jennie unfolded her arms and followed Lisa into the hall and down the stairs. She didn't like this. She didn't like it one bit. *Relax, McGrady*, her inner voice prompted. *It's just for one evening. You can handle anything for one night. Even a spoiled little rich girl like Allison Beaumont.*

2

When Lisa opened the door, Allison swept in, set down her sleeping bag and overnight case, and gave Lisa a hug. From what Lisa had said, Jennie expected the girl to be on the verge of hysteria. Instead, Allison seemed more fluttery and gracious than ever. Could be a cover-up, Jennie reminded herself. Allison was good at that.

"Thanks so much for your help," Allison gushed. Before Jennie could set her straight, Allison stepped away from Lisa and spread her arms out to Jennie. "You look great. And your tan—I am so jealous."

Jennie reluctantly allowed Allison to hug her, then stepped back. It was then she saw the girl standing on the porch. As if on cue, Allison turned and took the girl's hand and pulled her inside. "I'm sorry, where are my manners? This is Bethany, my . . . ah . . . sister. And these are my friends, Lisa Calhoun and Jennie McGrady."

"Hi." Bethany stuffed her hands into the pockets of her torn jeans. "And the name's B.J. Lewis. *Al*, here, seems to have a hearing problem."

"Bethany is a great name." Allison gave her sister a look Jennie suspected was a plea not to embarrass her.

"For you maybe. Not for me," B.J. argued.

You're right about that, Jennie felt like saying but

didn't. Bethany should have been sweet, maybe saintly. B.J. didn't fit the picture at all. Jennie shifted her gaze from one girl to the other. Talk about contrasts. Allison had fine features, clear skin, a small nose, and big blue eyes. Her straight, shoulder-length blond hair looked like she'd trained each strand to shimmer and sway in unison every time she moved her head. Alice in Wonderland and Cinderella all wrapped in one neat package.

B.J., on the other hand, had kinky brown hair and hazel eyes—sharp and piercing—the kind that made you feel as if she could see clear through to your soul. She was attractive, but next to Allison, her nose seemed a little too big, her hair a little too drab, and her clothes a little too shabby. Enough reason, Jennie decided, to like her.

"Look." B.J. took a step backwards. "I shouldn't be here. I told Al she didn't need to bring me, but she and Mrs. Beaumont insisted. I don't need to stay . . ."

"Don't be silly." Lisa stepped outside, grabbed B.J.'s bag, and brought it in the house. "There's always room for one more." She motioned B.J. in and closed the door behind them, then started up the stairs. "Let's put your stuff in Jennie's room, then we'll get some snacks and talk."

B.J. looked at Jennie as if waiting for her to second the motion. "Don't look at me." Jennie shrugged and grinned. "I just live here."

Interesting, Jennie mused as she took B.J.'s bag from Lisa and followed her up to her room. The canvas bag looked like a reject from Goodwill. B.J.'s clothes didn't look much better. Of course it was hard to tell these days when a pair of torn jeans sold at Nordstrom's for fifty dollars a pair. "Just toss the rest of your stuff over here," she said, pointing to the corner where she'd set B.J.'s bag.

"We'll sort out sleeping space later. So, B.J.," Jennie said as she ushered the party back downstairs, "I don't remember seeing you before. Do you live around here?"

"No."

When B.J. didn't offer any more information, Allison produced a nervous giggle. "A woman of few words. Actually, B.J. and our mother lived in California until . . ."

"Give it a rest, Al," B.J. muttered. "I'm sure Lisa and Jennie have more important things to do than listen to my life story. Why don't you cut the gab and get down to business? We all know you're not here for a social visit."

Allison stared openmouthed at her sister and, for the first time Jennie could remember, seemed at a loss for words. Part of her felt sorry for Allison, but the other part wanted to cheer B.J. on.

"C'mon," Jennie said as she led them into the kitchen. "Maybe we can find time for both." She pulled out the popcorn and air-popper and set them on the counter while Lisa raided the refrigerator for drinks.

B.J. hooked a leg over the barstool across the counter from Jennie. "I hear you're pretty good at solving mysteries. Think you can figure this one out?"

Jennie shrugged. "Which one, Allison's or yours?"

B.J. smiled and raised an eyebrow. "I'm not that hard to figure out."

"I think you are," Allison said.

"That's because you live such a sheltered life." B.J. shook her head. "You'd have a hard time understanding anybody whose house isn't worth a couple mil."

"That's not fair . . ." Allison began.

"It's true." Shifting her gaze from Allison to Jennie, B.J. added, "How about it, McGrady, think you can figure me out?"

16

"Come on, you guys," Lisa interrupted. She laughed nervously as she handed each of the girls a Coke. "I told you Jennie was a good detective, not a mind reader."

This is a test, pure and simple. But for what? *To determine whether or not I'm good enough to solve Allison's mystery? Or good enough to be a friend?* Whatever the reason, Jennie decided to accept the challenge.

"Maybe," Jennie answered as she reached into the cupboard for bowls. Then needing more time to think added, "But let's wait until we're upstairs. I do better with puzzles on a full stomach."

A few minutes later, the girls, carrying hot buttered popcorn, drinks, and a stash of chocolates, made their way from the kitchen, through the entry, and up the stairs to Jennie's room. Jennie and Lisa pulled a couple of over-stuffed chairs from their corner spaces and set them near the bed, then flopped onto it. Jennie set the popcorn on the floor so everyone could reach. B.J. sprawled onto the chair nearest Jennie. Allison sank into the other one and glanced at B.J. The look on Allison's face surprised Jennie. She'd expected the girl to be annoyed or embarrassed. What she saw was a kind of sadness—like maybe Allison felt sorry for B.J., or like she wanted to help but didn't know how.

"Okay, McGrady," B.J. said, interrupting Jennie's thoughts. She tossed a piece of popcorn in the air and caught it in her mouth. "Let's see how good you really are."

"You sure you want to do this?" Jennie asked. "I mean . . . I wouldn't want to embarrass you." The picture of B.J. forming in Jennie's mind was not a pleasant one and she wanted to give her an opportunity to back out.

B.J. leaned back in the chair and hooked a leg over the arm. "You can't embarrass me, McGrady. Now quit stalling."

"Okay, but just remember this was your idea." Jennie sighed, tossed a couple pieces of popcorn in her mouth, and began. "From the size of the chip you carry on your shoulder, I'd guess you've had a pretty rough life. You don't have much money, and you just recently discovered that you have a sister. Since Allison is older, I'd say your parents must have divorced before you were born. Allison grew up with her dad and his new wife, and you with your mom and maybe, since your last name is different, a stepfather."

B.J. stretched her legs out in front of her and leaned back. "Not bad. How'd you arrive at that?"

Jennie shrugged. "It wasn't really all that hard. You and Allison don't seem too comfortable together, so I figure you haven't known each other long. I just hooked together other pieces of information you gave me and things I noticed."

"That's fascinating," Allison injected.

"Not really. I know how you hate to be called Al. You haven't corrected her. That means you're still treading softly, not wanting to upset her. Besides, if she'd been around awhile, your folks wouldn't have made you bring her here tonight. And . . ." Jennie turned to B.J., ". . . your overnight bag is in pretty bad shape. That means Mrs. Beaumont hasn't had a chance to take you shopping."

"She offered. I refused."

Jennie nodded. "Which tells me something else. You're angry. Maybe at your mom for not telling you about your dad, or at your dad for not finding you sooner."

"I'm not mad at my mother. She's dead."

"You can still be mad at her." Jennie spoke from experience. As much as she loved her parents, especially her father, she had struggled with being angry at him for leaving and with her mother for giving up—for falling in love with Michael, and a lot of other things.

"Well, I'm not. Okay?" Bethany insisted. "My social worker found out about Mr. Beaumont being my father when we cleaned out the apartment where Mom and I lived."

Jennie twisted around to a sitting position and folded her legs in front of her. "So you started looking for him?"

"No. I didn't want to."

Her answer surprised Jennie, who'd give anything to know where her own father might be. "Why?" she asked.

"What do I need with a father? I'm nearly sixteen. I've practically been on my own since I was ten. Social services found him. At first he didn't believe them."

"You can't blame Daddy for that," Allison defended. "There are lots of people who would say they were related to us because we have money."

"Yeah, well I couldn't care less about his money," B.J. jeered. "I wouldn't be here at all if they hadn't threatened to put me in a foster home."

"I'm glad you're here. I always wanted a sister."

"I'll just bet. Anyway . . ." B.J. scooped up a handful of popcorn. "Let's just forget it. I'm sure these guys don't want to hear about our problems." To Jennie she said, "You're pretty good, McGrady." She hesitated a moment, then asked, "So, what do you think about Al's secret admirer?"

"It's probably a prank. Some old boyfriend with a grudge or maybe a sore loser." Jennie had another opinion but didn't voice it. If she had to choose a suspect at that moment, it would be B.J. Lewis.

"Not a chance. I'll bet this stalker doesn't even know Al. He probably read about her in the paper. I think we're dealing with a psycho here. I mean one day he's sending her flowers and love notes and the next he's threatening to kill her."

"Kill her?" Lisa and Jennie asked at the same time.

"You never told me he'd threatened to kill you," Lisa directed the accusation toward Allison.

"He hadn't . . . until today." Allison reached into the pocket of her cardigan, pulled out a square white envelope, and handed it to Lisa. "When I came home from church today I found this on my front porch along with . . ." Allison paused. Her voice broke.

"Dead roses," B.J. finished. "The guy sent her a dozen dead roses."

Lisa gasped as she read the note, then passed it to Jennie. The note, carefully written in bold block letters, read:

DEAD ROSES FOR A DEAD LADY

3

Jennie frowned as she handed back the note. "Did you call the police?"

Allison shook her head. "I didn't even tell my folks about it. What good would it do? The police just keep saying they'll look into it. All they ever do is ask a bunch of questions about my friends, take the evidence, and drive away."

Hugging a throw pillow she'd grabbed from the bed, Allison shifted her teary gaze from Lisa to Jennie. "I don't think they're taking this seriously. They say they're doing all they can, but . . ." She lifted a delicate hand to her eyes and brushed away the pooling tears. "Lisa says you might be able to help, Jennie. And I thought maybe . . ."

"Cut the waterworks, Al." B.J. leaned back in her chair and folded her arms in disgust. "My luck I'd be related to a crybaby." She turned to Jennie and said, "Look, McGrady, Lisa said you've solved a couple of mysteries. So what do you say? The cops are getting nowhere. Maybe between the four of us, we can flush this creep out."

Before Jennie could answer, the door to her bedroom burst open and a flash of red, white, and blue streaked in. "Popcorn! Yeah!" Nick leaped into the center of the group and stuck his fist into the popcorn bowl.

"Hey!" Jennie protested as she ruffled his hair. "This is a private party. You're supposed to knock, remember?"

Nick shrugged his shoulders. "But I smelleded the popcorn." He looked up at her, his deep blue eyes sparkling with excitement. "'Sides, I wanted to tell you 'bout the movie. It had this great big dog . . ." Nick spread his arms and deepened his voice. "This big. He had hair all over his eyes and this little girl was drowning and he jumped in and saved her." Nick paused for a breath.

"Sounds fascinating, but . . ." Jennie began.

"I want a dog just like him. I asked Mom and Michael and they said, 'We'll see.' "

"Sounds like *Beethoven*," B.J. offered.

Nick's huge eyes grew even wider as he glanced behind him, noticing for the first time that there were others in the room besides Lisa and Jennie. "Who are you?"

Lisa chuckled. "This is Allison and B.J. And this little cutie is Jennie's brother, Nick." Lisa pulled him up onto her lap and hugged him.

"Nick!" Mom called from the hallway. She stepped into Jennie's room. "There you are. I'm sorry, girls, he got away from me."

"That's okay." Jennie introduced B.J. and Allison to her mother.

"Oh, yes. Allison, I remember you from church. Your mother and I worked together on the clothing drive. Aren't you the Rose Festival Princess from Trinity High?"

Allison nodded.

"Congratulations. That's quite an honor."

"Thanks."

"Well, I'll let you girls get back to . . . whatever you

were doing. Come on, Nick. Let's go down and say good-night to Michael. He wants to read you a story before he goes."

"I sure do." Michael appeared in the doorway and settled an arm around Mom's shoulder. "How are you girls doing?"

Jennie felt like she'd been punched in the stomach. Michael had been around for several weeks now and Jennie didn't think she'd ever get used to his open affection for Mom. It just wasn't right. *I'd be fine if you weren't around*, Jennie wanted to say. Instead she offered a perfunctory "Okay" along with the others. Then in a supreme effort to be civil and to avoid a lecture from her mother, Jennie forced a smile and introduced the girls to Michael, then added, "I hear the movie was great."

"So was the pizza," Michael said, "but it would have been better if you'd been with us. Next time, okay?"

No. It is not okay. Aloud she said, "Sure."

"Hey, sport," Michael shifted his gaze to Nick, "better hurry or I'll eat all the ice cream."

Nick squirmed off Lisa's lap and scampered across the room. He paused just outside the door and peaked back in. "Jennie," he whispered, "can I have the popcorn?"

"You guys want any more?" With their round of no's, Jennie scooped up the still half full bowl and took it to him. She ushered him out with a promise that he could tell her all about the dog the next day.

Jennie dropped back onto the bed and tore open the bag of Hershey's Kisses.

"I didn't realize that was your mom, Jennie," Allison said. "I mean, you and Lisa are always together at church and I thought she was Lisa's mom . . . the red hair and all."

Lisa giggled. "People are always saying that. Actually, Aunt Susan, that's Jennie's mom, and my dad are brother and sister."

"And my aunt Kate is Lisa's mom," Jennie explained. "She and my dad are twins. I take after the McGrady side of the family and Lisa looks more like the Calhouns." She picked up the picture on her bedside table and showed it to them. "This is my dad."

"Then who was the guy with your mom? Are your folks divorced?" B.J. asked.

Jennie closed her eyes. It still hurt to think about it. "My dad disappeared five years ago. He was on a special assignment for the government when his plane went down in the Pacific. They never found him. Gram and I think he's still alive, but Mom's given up. She met Michael at church a few months ago, and now they're talking marriage."

"Bummer." B.J. handed back the picture. "My stepfather died when I was ten. Things sort of fell apart for Mom and me after that . . ." B.J. shifted and, as if she'd revealed too much, quickly changed the subject. "You don't look too happy about your mom getting married again."

Jennie gave B.J. a penetrating look. "Would *you* be?"

B.J. shrugged, looked at the photo and back at Jennie. "Have you tried to find him?"

"I'm working on it. My grandmother said she'd help me. We'll start the search as soon as she gets home. Unfortunately, I can't do much until then."

Allison leaned forward and extracted a piece of candy from the bag and peeled off the silver foil. "Lisa told me about your grandmother. She sounds fascinating. Traveling to all sorts of exotic places . . . and getting paid for it."

24

"I don't get it," B.J. said. "Why would you need your grandmother to search for your dad? Seems like an old person would just slow you down."

Lisa and Jennie exchanged a conspiratorial look and said in unison, "You don't know Gram."

"She used to be on the police force here in Portland," Lisa said. "Now she works for—"

"She writes . . ." Jennie interrupted, fearing Lisa would blab about Gram's connection with the FBI, ". . . for travel magazines. That's why she gets to travel so much. Sometimes she takes us along."

"Right." Lisa glanced at Jennie, indicating she'd gotten the message. "For our birthdays, Gram took Jennie to Florida and she's taking me on a cruise. I can hardly wait."

"She used to be a cop?" B.J. chewed on the edge of her thumbnail.

The way B.J. said it, Jennie wondered if the idea of being with a cop's granddaughters made her nervous. "Gram was a detective. Which is why I need her help." Jennie popped a second chocolate into her mouth. "Actually, I wish she were here now. She'd know what to do about Allison."

"You saying you can't work on Al's case without your grandmother?"

"No. It's just that Gram knows people. She has connections in the department."

Allison shook her head, setting her sleek blond hair in motion. "I don't think connections would help, Jennie. Dad has a lot of clout in this town. He's on the city council. It's not like the police aren't trying; they just haven't been able to come up with anything. That's why I talked with Lisa. I thought maybe we could do some investigating—I mean, four teenage girls might not pose a threat. . . . Please say you'll help, Jennie. I don't know how much longer I can take this."

Allison's voice faded. Her appeal hung on the air like a wintry mist, chilling the room.

Warnings rang again in Jennie's head. She could almost hear Gram saying, "This is a police matter, dear. Let them handle it." Still, it would be great to find the creep responsible for the threats and turn him over to the police. Part of her said, *You don't have enough experience for this kind of case.* Another argued, *It won't hurt to snoop around. Like Lisa said, you could just stay close to Allison and keep your eyes open.*

"Let me think about it," Jennie said, unwilling to say no, yet knowing that if Allison's stalker was as crazy as B.J. said, it could be dangerous for all of them.

"Well, think away, McGrady. You guys can sit here and play guessing games all night, but I'm going to turn in." B.J. yawned as she retrieved her bag from the end of the bed. "Where do you want us to sleep?"

Glad for the reprieve, Jennie hopped off the bed. "Anywhere you can find an empty space." Pointing to her window seat she added, "This is a nice spot. You can curl up on the cushions here if you want to. I do sometimes." Jennie removed a half dozen teddy bears in assorted sizes and colors and set them on the floor. When she got to the big white fluffy rabbit dressed in a Victorian pinafore, she paused and hugged it to her chest. "You're welcome to sleep with one if you want."

B.J. grinned. "Do I look like I need one?"

Jennie shrugged, closed the blind, and set the bunny against it. "Mom says we all do from time to time."

B.J. shook her head. "I don't need anything, Mc-

Grady." Pulling her toothbrush and toothpaste from her rumpled bag, she added, "Where's the bathroom?"

Jennie was about to answer when the phone rang. When she reached for the receiver, Allison stopped her. "No . . . don't answer it. It's him. I know it."

"Give it a rest, Al." B.J. came up behind them. "He wouldn't call here."

"B.J.'s right," Jennie said as she picked up on the third ring. "It's my private number—and it's unlisted." She put the phone to her ear and said, "Hello."

Jennie repeated herself several times. After a long silence the phone went dead. She replaced the receiver and looked from Lisa to B.J. to Allison. "They hung up."

"It was him. I knew it." Allison buried her face in her hands. "He must have followed me. He could be waiting out there right this minute!"

4

"Allison!" Jennie gripped her shoulders. "Calm down. We're safe here. It was probably a wrong number. Besides, if he were calling us he could hardly be waiting outside, could he?"

Allison's frailty gave Jennie a start. *Allison needs your help, McGrady.* Jennie dropped her hands and folded her arms. She did not want to help Allison. She didn't even like Allison. Actually, that wasn't quite true, Jennie realized. *Face it, McGrady, you're hooked and you know it.*

"Y-yes. He could." Allison drew away and sank back into the chair. "I think he has a cellular phone. There's usually static on the line when he calls. He won't talk if anyone but me answers. He must have followed me here."

Fear laced the edge of Jennie's spine. There had been static on the line—just like the kind you sometimes get from a mobile phone. "Okay, even if someone did follow you, how would he get my number?"

"Maybe he knows you too," B.J. offered. "He might be coming after you next. I saw this gruesome movie last week where this psycho stalked young girls, raped them, and cut . . ."

"Stop it!" Allison covered her mouth and closed her eyes.

Jennie didn't want to hear any more either. The more she got to know B.J., the more she suspected that this long lost relative was somehow involved in terrorizing Allison. If that were true, they both needed help.

"Look, if it will make you feel better, I'll take a look outside."

"Alone?" Lisa grabbed Jennie's arm. "I . . . I should go with you."

"I'll go," B.J. said in a tone that booked no opposition. "If we do run into the stalker, I think McGrady and I stand a better chance of taking him down."

"I resent that." Lisa, in a ready-to-fight stance, her fists balled and resting on her hips, looked up at B.J. The scene would have been laughable if the circumstances had been different.

B.J. had a strange glimmer of excitement in her eyes, as if she knew no one would be out there. Still, there was the small matter of the phone call. *A wrong number, McGrady,* Jennie reminded herself. *Just like you said. Or maybe B.J.'s accomplice?*

Jennie settled an arm on Lisa's shoulder. "You have to admit B.J. has a few pounds and inches on you. Which is why I think she should stay up here with Allison, while you and I have a look around."

"No way." B.J. glared at Jennie. "And I was beginning to think you had some brains."

"Lisa knows this neighborhood as well as her own. She and I will be able to tell right off if there's a car or person who doesn't belong here."

B.J. stood her ground, and for a moment Jennie was afraid the girl would deck her. She didn't. Instead, she backed off, a smirk on her face that read, *I've got you right where I want you.*

Jennie ignored it and motioned for Lisa to follow. When they reached the bottom of the stairway, she paused. Should she tell Mom and Michael about the phone call and Allison's suspicions? If there was someone out there, Michael would be able to protect them. *No,* her inner voice objected. *You don't need his help. You don't need him at all. Besides, there's probably no one out there anyway. . . . This is just a game B.J. has cooked up to give Allison and her folks a bad time.*

Putting a finger to her lips, Jennie signaled Lisa to slip out quietly. They crouched low and tiptoed past the living room where Mom and Michael snuggled on the couch, watching an old movie on television. *Casablanca.* Jennie had seen it half a dozen times with Gram. Maybe if Jennie got lucky, Michael would take a hint from Humphrey Bogart. Dad would show up and Michael would tip his hat and say goodbye to Mom. "Here's lookin' at you, kid," he'd say and get into his BMW and drive off into the sunset. Then Mom and Dad would walk arm in arm into the house. Unfortunately, Michael didn't look like the Bogey type. She had a hunch he related himself more closely to the hero who always got the girl. Jennie pushed the depressing thoughts aside and concentrated instead on getting out of the house unnoticed.

Jennie and Lisa reached the entry and carefully let themselves out. Once the door was closed, Jennie suggested they separate.

"Not a chance," Lisa whispered, grabbing hold of Jennie's sleeve. "I think we should go together." Jennie started to object, then agreed. She had to admit, if there was someone hanging around out there, they'd be safer as a pair.

They began to circle the house. As they approached

the back, Jennie held an arm out to stop Lisa. "Shh. I think I heard something." Jennie peaked around the corner into the backyard. She'd never noticed it before, but if someone wanted to spy on her, they could easily do so from the massive maple tree that stood only a few feet from the house. Someone could climb the tree and look directly into her bedroom window. The limbs swayed now with the evening breeze. Or was the movement caused by something or someone else?

The stalker could be there right now, fully hidden by the heavy foliage. She eased back and rubbed her arms to chase away the chill. *Stop it, McGrady! No one's up there. This thing has got you spooked. You're doing exactly what B.J. wants you to do.*

"What is it?" Lisa whispered. "Did you see something?"

Jennie shook her head and took a deep breath. "No. I . . ." she started to tell Lisa about the tree, then stopped. "It's just the wind." *No sense worrying her*, Jennie decided. No sense taking chances either. If someone was hiding in the tree, she had no intention of getting near it. "There's no one back here," she said. "Let's check the other side."

They doubled around to the other side of the house. Nothing seemed out of place or unusual. "Let's go back in," Jennie suggested.

"Not yet." Lisa pulled on Jennie's arm, urging her onto the sidewalk. "I think we ought to go around the block. The guy could be parked somewhere nearby."

Jennie shrugged and walked along. "Okay, but we're wasting our time. If you want my opinion, B.J. is behind this whole thing."

"That's impossible. She was with us tonight. She

couldn't have made that phone call."

"I know, but it's possible the call was a wrong number or that B.J. is working with someone. You saw how she acted in there. She didn't seem the least bit scared. I think she knows we won't find anything. Why do you think she was so keen on coming with me?"

"But the phone calls and flowers started before B.J. moved in with the Beaumonts."

"That doesn't mean she couldn't have done it. Think about it. B.J. told us she didn't want to come. She also said her father didn't want her at first. She could have found out about Allison and started harassing her before she moved up here."

"You're right, it does seem like she enjoys seeing Allison suffer. But why?"

"Jealousy." Jennie stopped and hunkered down to tie a shoelace that had come undone. "We don't know the whole story, but think about it. Allison is rich and has everything she's ever wanted. B.J.'s poor and has practically had to take care of herself. I could be wrong, but she might have been abused. That could screw her up emotionally." Jennie straightened and started walking again.

"Yeah," Lisa said, "like the woman who came to talk to our youth group a couple of months ago. You remember. Her dad had abused her. She used to think about killing him and killing herself. She was into drugs and alcohol and just about everything else before getting into the counseling program at church."

They walked in silence until they'd circled back to Magnolia Street, where Jennie lived. Nothing seemed out of place in the quiet neighborhood except for Hannah Stuart's tricycle. The four-year-old, whom Jennie sometimes baby-sat, had left it on the sidewalk again. Jennie picked it up and deposited it near their front porch. The Stuarts lived at the end of the block. Next to them were the Murrays, an older couple, then the Whites, Jennie's next-door neighbors. With the exception of Allison's dark green convertible, all the cars were parked off the street in their respective driveways.

"Look!" Lisa pointed to a car parked in the Murrays' driveway. "I don't remember seeing that car around here before—did they get a new one?"

"Strange," Jennie said, walking toward it. "Mr. and Mrs. Murray left for California last week. Their daughter is having a baby and they said they'd be gone a month. No one should be here."

"Maybe they asked someone to house sit or water the plants," Lisa suggested.

"Uh-uh," Jennie shook her head. "Mom's doing that. We'd better get back to the house and call the police."

"Why don't we check out the car first? This could be the guy who's after Allison." Lisa hurried toward the car and peaked in the window. "Jennie," she squeaked, "there's a cellular phone."

Jennie came up beside her and tugged at her arm to get her out of there. "A lot of people have cellular phones. Come on, Lisa. Whoever owns this car could be burglarizing the house this minute. We've got to call the police."

Click. A metallic sound echoed in the still night air. Jennie froze.

"Back away from the car," a menacing voice ordered. "Now!"

5

"Do what he says," Jennie whispered. "He has a gun."

A strangled gasp escaped Lisa's throat. Jennie eased away from the car, trying to keep Lisa behind her. Slowly, she turned toward the voice.

She didn't see him at first. Then as he waved the gun, the streetlight reflected off the barrel. He stood at the corner of the house, partially hidden by a large lacy-leaf maple. "If you two want to live to see another sunrise," he rasped, "you'd better get out of here."

Jennie grabbed Lisa's hand and ran, stopping only when they had reached the safety of Jennie's yard. Jennie took a deep breath to steady her erratic heartbeat. "Go on in," she whispered to Lisa. "Call 911 and tell Mom what's going on. I'll be there in a minute."

"What are you going to do?"

"I just want to see if I can get a better look at him or maybe get the license number."

"No, don't go . . ."

Lisa's plea faded as Jennie hurried back to the Murray place. This time, however, she stayed under cover of the shrubs. As she reached their lawn, the car's motor roared to life. The intruder backed out of the driveway and tore down the street, burning rubber as the tires squealed around the corner. Jennie stomped her feet and turned back, nearly colliding with Michael.

"Are you okay?" he asked. "Lisa called the police. They should be here any minute. You'd better come inside where it's safe."

"He's gone. I tried to get a look at the license number, but even with the streetlight it was too dark to see much."

"What were you two doing out here alone? You shouldn't have gone back there. You could have been killed," Michael admonished as they walked back to her house.

So who died and made you king? Jennie bit her lip and held back the caustic remark. "I just wanted to . . . never mind. You're right. It was a stupid thing to do."

"Not stupid . . . let's just call it an unhealthy choice." Michael reached out as if he wanted to put an arm around her shoulders, then, apparently changing his mind, reached up to rub the back of his neck. "So, did you see anything?"

Before she could answer, Lisa, Allison, B.J., and Mom spilled out of the house and ran toward them. At the same time a squad car, with lights flashing and sirens wailing, pulled up to the curb in front of their house. Two police officers jumped out. "You the people who called about a prowler?"

The officer directed his question at Michael, but Jennie answered. She and Lisa filled them in on the car and the gunman and were surprised at how much they actually remembered. The car was a newer model—metallic gray, with gray interior, fancy spoke hubcaps and whitewall tires. Jennie closed her eyes trying to remember every detail like Gram had taught her. "Envision it," Gram had said. "Let the scene flow back into your mind. You'd be surprised at how much you can recall."

"It had Oregon plates," Jennie said. "Two zeros on the end." She envisioned the gun pointing at them. He'd been holding it away from him, arms stretched. Jennie mimicked the stance and raised her arms, letting her fingers take the form of a gun. He'd aimed the gun down at her chest, which would make the gunman just a little taller than her own height.

Jennie related her observations to the officers and pointed to the one whose name pin read Greg Donovan. "He was about your height and build."

When Jennie and Lisa had finished their report, one of the officers, a tall, dark-haired Hispanic named Tony Mendoza, left to radio in the report.

While he was gone, Officer Donovan smiled at Jennie and Lisa. "You kids did a great job. You're very observant."

Jennie flushed while Lisa gave him a wide smile and said, "Our grandmother used to be a police detective. Maybe you know her—Helen McGrady?"

"You're kidding," Greg's grin broadened. "McGrady's your grandmother? Hey, we worked together a couple times when I was a rookie. Tell her hi from me when you see her."

When Mendoza returned, the two officers got the Murrays' key from Mom, then she and Michael went with them to check out the house to see if the guy had gotten away with anything.

"You girls go on inside and lock the door," Mom said before she left. "We'll be back in a few minutes. And, Jennie, you'd better check on Nick."

Once inside, Jennie sent Lisa into the kitchen with

Allison and B.J. to make hot chocolate. She ran upstairs to Nick's room and made her way through building blocks, trucks, and cars to his bed. Smiling, she removed the book he'd fallen asleep with . . . *I'll Love You Forever*. His favorite. It was about a mother's love for her son. The story made Jennie cry whenever she read it.

Jennie pulled a sheet and light blanket over him, kissed his cheek, and turned out the lamp. The night-light cast a surrealistic glow over the room. "Sleep tight, little buddy," she whispered. He'd be disappointed when he learned he'd slept through all the excitement, but it was just as well. It would have taken forever to get him back to sleep.

Jennie took the stairs two at a time and headed for the kitchen. Lisa was in the middle of her detailed explanation of what had happened.

"I can't believe you actually looked in the window." Allison reached for the hot, steamy mug Lisa handed her. "Weren't you scared?"

"I guess I didn't think about it. I wanted to see if the guy had a cellular phone. I mean . . . I never dreamed he'd show up with a gun."

"Do you think he's the stalker?" Allison asked.

"I doubt it," Jennie answered. "Obviously the guy's a burglar. The fact that he has a cellular phone is just a coincidence."

"How can you be so sure?" B.J. asked as she crossed her ankles, leaned against the refrigerator, and took a sip of hot chocolate.

"Just a hunch."

Lisa handed Jennie a cup. "Doesn't it seem odd to you that he would pick tonight? That he'd have a cellular phone *and* be positioned in a spot where he could look right into your bedroom window?"

Jennie's heart plummeted. Lisa was right. From her side-yard window, she had an unobstructed view of Mr. and Mrs. Murray's driveway. *He could have been watching the whole time.*

"You know, McGrady, Lisa could have something there." B.J. looked entirely too pleased with herself.

Jennie felt like calling B.J.'s bluff. The man was a burglar. Couldn't they see that? While she debated about whether or not to confront her, the phone rang. Jennie answered.

"Hi, stranger," the faraway voice said. The evening's activities and concerns scurried out of her mind like gray mice into a black hole. She smiled and hugged the phone closer, suddenly breathless and flushed.

"Ryan. How are you? How's the fishing?" *When are you coming home? I miss you like crazy.* She didn't say the last part out loud. It had been too long and their relationship wasn't far enough along. Ryan's summer job had taken him on a fishing boat in Alaska. It still rankled Jennie that he'd gone.

"Great. I tried to call you earlier, but all I got was a bunch of static. When I finally got it to ring, no one answered. I was about ready to give up when I remembered you guys had two lines, so I decided to try this one."

"That was you?" Relief flooded her. Jennie glanced up at the others who were watching and listening to the one-sided exchange with rapt interest. Jennie quickly explained about Allison and the stalker and how they'd thought the phone call might have been from him.

After telling her to be careful, Ryan hesitated. "Ah, Jennie," he continued, "I've got some good news and some bad news."

This is it, McGrady. He's dumping you. He's found a girl in Alaska . . . Jennie didn't want to hear Ryan's bad news but listened anyway.

"The good news," Ryan said, "is that by the end of the summer I'll have made enough money to get me through the first two years of college. The bad news, for us anyway, is that I've signed on for another month—at least. Looks like I'll have to break our date for the end of this month."

This wasn't fair. Jennie turned away from her rapt audience and leaned against the kitchen wall. She finally found a guy she really cared about and all he cared about was making money. *That's not entirely true, McGrady,* a voice in her head argued, but she ignored it.

"Jennie? Are you still there?"

Jennie took a deep breath, hoping to hold back the menacing tears that threatened to break through her resolve. "I'm here. Just disappointed. I was looking forward to . . . never mind. I hope everything goes really well for you." Then something terrible happened. Jennie's thoughts merged with her tongue. Before she could stop them, the angry words had escaped. "In fact, you can stay there all summer if you want. Just don't expect me to be here when you come back."

Neither of them spoke for what seemed like an eternity. Finally, Ryan broke the silence. "That was a low blow, McGrady. I thought. . . . Listen, I have to go. Some of the other guys are waiting to use the phone. I'll try to call you sometime next week."

"Don't bother." After Jennie hung up, she wanted to crawl into the woodwork and disappear. Misery was too pale a word for what she felt. On top of that her guests had overheard every word. She did not look forward to having to explain.

Thankfully, when she turned around, Lisa, Allison, and B.J. were huddled together around the kitchen table talking about the stalker. *Bless you, Lisa.* Jennie stood behind Allison and B.J. and mouthed a grateful "thank you" to her cousin.

"You can relax, Allison," Jennie announced. "Our mysterious caller was Ryan. He had a bad connection." *Unfortunately, the second one wasn't that great either.*

"I'm just glad he didn't get in," Mom said as she entered the kitchen through the back door.

"Looks like you girls surprised the prowler before he had a chance to break in," Officer Mendoza offered when Jennie asked what they'd found. A few minutes later, Mendoza and Donovan thanked everyone for their help and left. The girls washed out their mugs and headed back upstairs.

An hour later, Jennie was still awake, only it wasn't the burglary that haunted her. *You messed up good this time, McGrady. Ryan may never speak to you again.* "What am I going to do, God?" she whispered. "I love Ryan so much. What if he won't forgive me?" Alongside that thought came another. *What if he will?* The more she considered the possibility, the more it made sense. Ryan had been a friend for a lot longer than he'd been a boyfriend. She'd write to him and explain how hurt she'd felt, how disappointed and angry—not at him, but at the circumstances keeping them apart. Knowing she wouldn't be able to fall asleep until she'd accomplished her task, Jennie decided to write the letter right away.

She eased open her nightstand drawer and pulled out some stationery and a pen. Twenty minutes and five sheets of paper later she signed her final draft, stuffed it into an envelope, and leaned it against her lamp. She returned the paper and pen to the drawer and snapped off the light.

Still unable to sleep, Jennie eased out of bed and slipped a cream-colored cotton throw over her shoulders. She made her way across the clothes-littered floor, around the bodies sleeping there, and raised the blinds of the window facing the Murrays' house. The driveway was empty, but it didn't take much imagination to envision the car and the driver sitting there watching. *That's just super, McGrady. Now you're getting paranoid too.*

She lowered the blinds and tiptoed back to her bed. She'd just pulled up the covers when the phone rang. She grabbed for it before it could ring again, hoping it would be Ryan so she could apologize right then and there.

"Hello," she answered.

The line hissed and crackled with static. No one answered.

"Ryan?" Jennie spoke in a loud whisper, not wanting to wake the others.

"Jennie McGrady," the distorted voice broke through the noise on the line. "Shame on you for calling the cops on me. Too bad for you I got away."

Threads of fear laced through Jennie's stomach and tightened their hold. "Who is this?" Jennie closed her eyes and swallowed back the panic rising in her chest.

"Ask Allison." He chuckled. "And tell her she can't escape. Wherever she goes, whatever she does, I'll be there. And if you and that snoopy cousin of yours try to stop me, I'll get you too."

6

"Come on, Jennie, wake up," Lisa insisted. "Allison and B.J. have already gone. They said to tell you thanks. Allison had to go shopping for the party."

Somewhere between two and three in the morning, Jennie had managed to fall asleep. That meant, according to her fuzzy calculations, she'd only slept about four hours.

"Good," she groaned. "You leave too so I can go back to sleep."

"You don't have time for that. We have to develop a game plan for how we're going to catch the guy who's been stalking Allison."

Memories of the gunman and the early morning phone call zapped into Jennie's mind, ridding her of all desire for sleep. She bolted out of bed. Sometime during the night, whether it was the call itself or the realization that the caller knew her name and had held a gun on her and Lisa, Jennie had made a decision. Like it or not, she was involved and intended to solve the mystery of Allison Beaumont's stalker and put him behind bars.

She told Lisa about the one a.m. phone call.

"So it *was* him." Lisa looked pleased with herself. "I knew it. I guess that blows your theory about Bethany."

"B.J.," Jennie corrected. "And no, it doesn't. It just means she could be working with someone."

"Why are you so sure she's involved? Just because she's had a rough life doesn't mean she's a criminal."

"I know that. But Gram says in an investigation you have to suspect everyone—even Allison. It wouldn't be the first time someone has set things up to make themselves look like a victim. Look at all the publicity this has gotten her."

"You really think that's all this is . . . a publicity stunt?" Lisa frowned. "Now that I think about it, Allison has gotten a lot of attention. You think she hired someone?"

"It's possible. What we need to look for is motive and opportunity. Allison has always wanted to sing. This could get her the attention she needs to launch her career." Pleased with the direction her thoughts had taken, Jennie pursued the idea. "If Allison is guilty she has to be working with someone. Who's she dating now?"

"I'm not sure. With all the Rose Festival activities I don't think she's had much time for guys."

"Well, we'd better start our investigation with Allison and B.J. We need to ask questions and keep our eyes open." Jennie picked up a hairbrush and began working out the snarls in her hair. "Let's start with B.J. What do you know about her? She made any close friends here?"

"I don't think so." Lisa pushed one of the chairs back into its corner and plopped into it. "She's only been around for about three weeks. And she's not exactly winning any points with people."

Jennie nodded, then sighed. "Okay. Call Allison. Tell her we'll help. See if we can stay at her house tonight. We'll help her get ready for her party tomorrow and have a look around."

"I thought you weren't going."

Jennie grimaced. "Much as I hate the idea, I think it's probably the best way to find clues and dig up the latest gossip—and find out who Al's friends and enemies are. At the same time we need to learn all we can about B.J.—who she talks to and if she has any guys hanging around."

Lisa bounced out of the chair and started pacing. "I hate to think that guy last night could be someone we know. Or that one of my friends would pull a gun on us."

"There are a lot of kids we don't know all that well," Jennie reminded her as she set the hairbrush aside and headed for her bed. She pulled up the sheets, adjusted the comforter, and tossed the pillows into place. "Besides, remember that discussion we had in political science when Barry Owen's father talked to us about gun-control legislation? About half the class thought people should have a right to bear arms. A few even admitted they had purchased guns to protect themselves." The thought of some of those kids carrying guns sent chills shuddering down Jennie's spine. She'd seen firsthand what a bullet could do and didn't want anything to do with them.

"You're right. I'd forgotten about that." Lisa grabbed Jennie's arm. "I just remembered! Allison's dad has a gun collection. I saw it last year at her party when he took some of us on a tour of the house."

"All the more reason to stay there tonight. I'd like to have a look at it." Excitement soared through Jennie, lifting her mood and her spirits. She imagined herself waiting until everyone in the house was asleep . . . then she'd sneak down the wide circular staircase, into the massive kitchen, and down the basement steps. She'd use the key to the wine cellar, which she would have confiscated earlier from the butler.

Jennie would glance around her to make certain no one had followed, then step into the damp, dark cellar and brush away the cobwebs. There in the beam of her flashlight would be . . . a skeleton. *No . . . no . . . no. This is a modern mansion, not a haunted castle in Ireland. The gun case, McGrady, get back to the gun case.* Jennie imagined a massive gun case covering the back wall. In the lower right-hand corner where an antique gun should have been—the one Billy the Kid had used—there'd be nothing but an indentation and an I.D. plaque.

She'd gather all the suspects into the living room, just like Detective Poirot in the Agatha Christie mysteries, and then bring the missing gun to Mr. Beaumont's attention and confront Allison. It would be Allison, Jennie decided, not B.J. It was always the least likely suspect.

You did it, didn't you, Allison? she'd say. *I suspected you all along. What I couldn't figure out was who was working with you. Now I know that too. There's only one answer. Only one person had the key to the gun case. Only one person knew the old gun still worked. And only one person had the ammunition. It was you, Mr. Beaumont. You wanted your daughter to succeed. You—*

"Jennie?" Lisa's voice interrupted her fantasy. "Earth calling Jennie . . . come in, Jennie."

"What. . . ?"

"Where were you? I hate it when you space out like that. It gives me the creeps."

"I'm sorry. I was just thinking about the gun case. Lisa, do you remember much about the gun the guy was using last night?"

"No. Do you?"

"Just that it was silver and had a long barrel. It reminded me of the kind of revolvers they used in old cowboy movies." The phone rang. It was Aunt Kate—calling to remind Lisa about her tennis lessons. A few minutes later Lisa left, promising to call Allison and set things up for that night.

Jennie finished cleaning her room, took a shower, dressed, then headed downstairs for a late breakfast. Mom was just finishing the dishes. "Good morning. I saved you some scrambled eggs and bacon."

"Thanks." Jennie placed the cooled breakfast into the microwave and turned it on.

Mom plopped a piece of bread into the toaster, then asked, "Want some toast?"

"Do I have a choice?" Jennie asked, grinning as she nodded toward the toaster.

"Oh." Mom laughed. "Habit. You don't have to eat it."

"Do we have any freezer jam?"

"Sure." She retrieved a plastic container from the fridge. "Your favorite. Raspberry."

The microwave beeped and Jennie rescued the steamy, slightly overcooked eggs and sat at the kitchen table.

"Jennie . . ."

Uh-oh. Here it comes. She's going to ask about last night. Might as well get it over with. "Look Mom, about last night—"

"Oh, yes, wasn't it awful. . . . I mean, imagine a burglar right here in our own quiet little neighborhood. It's a good thing no one was hurt."

"Aren't you going to yell at me for being outside?"

"No," she said, pouring herself a cup of coffee. "But I would like to know why you went out without telling me."

Jennie debated about whether or not to tell her the truth. Then decided she'd better. The last time she'd lied to her mother, she'd nearly gotten herself, Gram, and Ryan killed. Mom joined Jennie at the table, and Jennie dutifully filled her mother in on the details of the case while she ate.

"Anyway," Jennie concluded, "it looks like the guy Lisa and I saw last night is Allison's stalker. I'm going to let the police know about the call after breakfast. Lisa and I thought we'd hang out with Allison for the next few days, see if maybe we can help."

"I can't believe this. I remember when we used to be able to leave our doors unlocked at night. Now you can't turn on the news without hearing about something horrible. And now . . . a stalker in our own neighborhood. And poor Allison. She must be frantic."

"Lisa and I were planning on spending the night with Allison to help her get ready for the party tomorrow. Is that okay with you?"

Mom blinked and gave Jennie a blank stare that seemed to say, *Are you crazy?*

Well, that's it, McGrady. Looks like you won't be going to the party after all. Part of her was relieved that she wouldn't be going, but part of her had been looking forward to working on the case.

"Yes, Allison's mother already spoke with me this morning," Mom said. "Even though the Beaumonts assured me you girls would be well cared for, my first inclination was to say no. I didn't want you anywhere near that family. But that wouldn't be fair to Allison or to you. She really needs friends around her right now, doesn't she?"

Mom caressed her cup, then a moment later, set it

down on the table so hard the coffee sloshed out. "Besides that, I am not going to let some criminal turn us into frightened rabbits who are afraid to cross the street without a police escort. No criminal is going to dictate our lives." She pulled a couple napkins out of the holder and mopped up the brown liquid before it could run onto the floor.

"Mom?" Few things got her mother riled, but when they did, Susan McGrady went into action. The way she went from mild-mannered bookkeeper to political activist reminded Jennie of Wonder Woman. "You're not going to do anything weird, are you?"

"Of course not. But I am going to call the police and schedule a neighborhood meeting. We need to be prepared." She placed her arms on the table and leaned forward. "Jennie, I won't keep you from spending time with Allison, but promise me you won't do anything foolish."

Annoyed at the direction the conversation was taking, Jennie asked, "What's that supposed to mean?"

"It means, I don't want you trying to capture this guy by yourself. If you notice anything unusual, tell the police."

"I'm not stupid." Jennie pushed away from the table, scooped up her dishes, and took them to the sink to rinse them off.

"I know, but you do have a knack for getting into trouble."

"Nothing's going to happen."

Mom rose from the table and set her cup in the dishwasher. "I'm sorry if I seem critical. It's just that you're the only daughter I have. If anything ever happened to you . . ." She put an arm around Jennie and hugged her.

Jennie hugged her back. "We'll be fine." When she

drew away, she decided to change the subject before Mom changed her mind. "Listen, I cleaned my room. Did you want me to do the laundry or anything?"

"Maybe when you get back."

Jennie frowned. "Back from where? I'm not going anywhere until late this afternoon."

"Don't you remember? You have an appointment with Gloria at eleven. That gives you . . ." Mom checked her watch, "about thirty minutes to get ready."

Jennie groaned and headed upstairs to her room. The last thing she wanted to do was see a counselor. Just thinking about it brought back a rush of feelings Jennie didn't want to deal with. Anger at Mom for giving up and pushing her to accept Dad's death. Anger at Michael for asking Mom to marry him. Frustration that she had so little time. And fear that she, even with Gram's help, might not be able to find Dad.

A few weeks ago Mom had insisted that Jennie see the same counselor she had been seeing. Gloria had said Jennie needed to "work on grief issues over losing your father." They wanted to send her to a counseling camp for teens with similar problems. Problems, ha. The only problem Jennie had was with the counseling.

So far, except for her first appointment with Gloria, Jennie had managed to escape counseling camp, but sometime this summer, she'd have to go. She'd promised Mom, and it was either that or risk being grounded for the rest of her life. The same was true of the individual counseling sessions. Jennie hoped Gloria would realize that she didn't need help and that the counseling camp would be a waste of time.

Since she stubbornly refused to acknowledge her dad's death, Jennie doubted that her reprieve would come anytime soon.

An hour and a half later, Jennie backed out of her parking place and drove away from the counseling center. She'd decided to be totally honest this time around. No games, no pretending. She even told Gloria about the box in her closet marked "Dad's Things," which she took down and examined whenever she got to feeling lonely or depressed. And the journal in which she wrote letters to him.

To Jennie's surprise, Gloria had said, "What a wonderful idea! It helps keep his memory close."

Her response had softened Jennie a little. At least Gloria didn't think she was totally bonkers. In fact, Jennie realized, when it was time to go, the session hadn't been too bad. Gloria had praised her for being honest about her feelings. The thing that impressed Jennie most was that Gloria hadn't tried to convince her Dad was dead. In fact, Jennie wondered if maybe she had convinced Gloria that Dad really was still alive.

When Jennie got to the main road, instead of heading home she made a left. Since she was only a mile or so away from the Lakeside development where Allison lived, she figured it wouldn't hurt to drive by.

Jennie turned on to Lakeview Drive and checked the addresses. She'd only seen Allison's house a couple of times, when the kids had car pooled to youth meetings. She had no trouble spotting the Beaumont home, though. The mansionlike structure was set back from the road on a knoll overlooking the lake. Some six acres of perfectly landscaped lawn set it apart from the other homes, making it look like an island in a sea of green. Jennie felt suddenly shy and, instead of pulling into the driveway, parked across the street.

You don't belong here, McGrady, a voice in her head insisted. She glanced down at her faded cutoffs and dark green University of Oregon T-shirt, then looked at the house, the yard . . . heck, it wasn't even a yard, it was an estate. Intimidating, she decided. As much as she loved her little car, driving the five-year-old Mustang into Allison's driveway would be like . . .

"Stop it, McGrady," Jennie said aloud, shaking her head. "You're being ridiculous. Just because they have money doesn't make them any better than you."

It didn't, of course. Still, something about people who lived in glamorous houses made Jennie uncomfortable. Before she could formulate a reason for her discomfort, an off-white van drove up behind her and made a left turn into the Beaumonts' driveway. *Tricia's Flowers*, the bold, black letters read. A bouquet of roses had been painted behind the letters in shades of red. The driver pulled up to the front door, got out, and retrieved a box from the back of the van before knocking on the door. No one must have answered because he left the box, hopped in his van, and drove away.

Jennie waited until he was out of sight, then drove up to the house. Looking around and seeing no one, she crept up to the front door and, feeling brave, nudged the lid off the box with the toe of her sneaker.

Nestled in lavender tissue paper and lying in a crisp white box lay a beautiful bouquet of pink rosebuds, with sprays of baby's breath and delicate ferns. Jennie hunkered down in front of the box and picked up the flowers to get a closer look at the card tacked to the pink bow.

"Hold it right there," a voice behind her thundered.

7

Jennie clutched the roses to her chest and turned, fully expecting to be looking down the barrel of another gun. Instead she found herself looking at a garden rake. Well, not at the rake exactly, but at the guy leaning on it. He was tan, no—make that bronze—with penetrating blue eyes and long golden hair, which he'd pulled back into a ponytail.

"Who are you?" she managed to croak out as she zeroed in on a spot behind him and tried not to stare.

"I think that's my line." His mouth parted to reveal a perfect set of white teeth. "Name's Rocky. I work here. You, on the other hand, appear to be trespassing."

"Jennie. I—I'm Jennie, a friend of Allison's."

He shifted his gaze from her eyes to the package she held in her arms. "Friend? I don't think so."

Jennie's mouth dropped open. He suspected her. He thought *she'd* delivered the flowers and that she was the stalker. "I . . . this isn't . . ."

"Save it. Beaumont ought to be back any minute now. You can explain it to him."

Rocky let the rake fall into a large juniper and stepped onto the porch. He wasn't much taller than Jennie but still seemed to dwarf her. She backed up, trapping herself between him and the house.

Rocky took hold of her arm and was about to usher her inside the house when a silver Mercedes pulled into the driveway. Mr. Beaumont stepped out of the car and walked toward them. Her heart pounded a thunderous rhythm in her brain as she watched him approach. *Nice going, McGrady. You just couldn't stay out of it, could you? That package could be from the stalker, and now it's got your prints all over it.*

"What's going on here?" Mr. Beaumont asked, shifting his gaze from Rocky to Jennie.

"I caught her trying to deliver these flowers."

Mr. Beaumont frowned. "Is this true?"

"No . . . of course not." Jennie closed her eyes and shook her head. "This is crazy. I'm Jennie McGrady. Allison stayed at my house last night. She seemed pretty shook up. I was just driving by to see how she was doing when I saw a van drive in with these. I thought I'd check it out . . ."

"A van?" Rocky and Mr. Beaumont said together. "What kind of van?" Mr. Beaumont asked. "Think carefully, Jennie. What did it look like?" Apparently both men had dismissed her as a suspect, and that was just fine with her.

Jennie described the van in as much detail as she could. When she'd finished, Rocky left, saying he'd call it in. "Here." Jennie handed the flowers to Mr. Beaumont. "You'd better take these. I hope I didn't mess up anything. Just wanted to get a look at the card."

Beaumont slid the card from its square white envelope, read it, and handed it to Jennie. *Hi, Princess*, it read. *You reign in my heart.*

"This doesn't sound threatening—you think it's from the guy who's been stalking Allison?" Jennie handed the card back.

"I suspect it is. The first couple of deliveries were like this. He's either trying to throw us off the track, or we're dealing with a very disturbed person."

Or a daughter who needs attention, Jennie thought. *And both Allison and B.J. fit the picture.*

Beaumont nodded silently, and Jennie took his action as a dismissal. "I'd better go. Tell Allison and B.J. I came by. I'll be back later this afternoon."

He shook her hand, acting cool and aloof. "I'm sorry if Rocky frightened you. Part of his job around here is to keep an eye on the place."

"It's okay. I understand how it must have looked."

"Yes," he said, walking her to her car. "Jennie, I want you to know that Allison and B.J.'s friends are welcome here, anytime. But I suggest you call ahead from now on. It could save us from this kind of embarrassment."

As she drove toward home, Jennie tried to review the incident objectively. Something bothered her about the Beaumonts' gardener. On the surface it made sense. The gardener catching a kid who didn't belong there . . . but a gardener? He looked more like a model.

Jennie pulled into her driveway. Her mother, decked out in cutoffs, a halter top, a wide-brimmed hat, and garden gloves, waved from the flower garden bordering the front of the house. Jennie grinned—Mom looked like she'd been in a fight with a dirt clod and lost.

That's it! A real gardener would have been grungy—he would have at least had dirt on his hands. Jennie glanced at her watch. By this time of the day, with the temperature rising toward ninety degrees, he would have been sweaty too. Rocky had looked like he'd stepped out of the pages of a *GQ* magazine, not a garden. *Still,* Jennie reminded herself, *Mr. Beaumont did say Rocky had other jobs. He could have just gotten started on the gardening.*

Somehow Jennie doubted that. Most gardeners she knew worked early in the day. Besides, her intuition told her that Rocky wasn't what he seemed. Her mind skittered back to the night before—to the man with the gun. Could Rocky be the stalker? Could he have won Mr. Beaumont's confidence and gotten himself this job to be close to Allison? Jennie shuddered at the thought and added his name to her growing list of suspects.

"Lisa called a few minutes ago," Mom hollered as Jennie opened the car door and stepped out. "She said it was urgent." Mom laughed. "'Course with Lisa, everything is urgent." She leaned back on her heels and wiped an arm across her forehead, leaving another dirt stain on her face. "How was your session with Gloria?"

"Okay, but I still think it's a waste of money to make me go." Jennie stopped at the porch steps and leaned against the white pillar. "Mom, how well do you know the Beaumonts?"

Mom gave her a don't-change-the-subject look, but answered anyway. "Not well, really. Janet—Allison's mother—and I have worked on a couple of church projects, but that's about it. She seems like a very nice person. Homey, warm, generous. I understand they're one of the church's biggest supporters. Why do you ask?"

"Just curious." Jennie lowered herself to the step. "What about Mr. Beaumont?"

"Well, he's on the church board. From what Michael says, he's a great guy. In fact it was David Beaumont who suggested Michael intern at Trinity."

"What do you mean?" Jennie frowned, as a knot began to form at the pit of her stomach. Something told her she wasn't going to like Mom's answer one bit. "I thought Michael was a building contractor," she added, remembering the time he'd taken them by a house he'd built.

"He is, but that's only part time. You remember, Jennie, he told you he was going to school. He's been studying at the seminary for the past three years, and now he's ready to do his internship. Mr. Beaumont talked the church board into hiring Michael as the new youth director."

The knot in Jennie's stomach exploded. "The youth director? Oh, that's just great. How could he do that to me? How humiliating! Why don't you guys just strip me naked and hang me by my toenails in Pioneer Square?"

"Jennie, don't be ridiculous." Mom stood up and brushed the dirt off her knees. "What's gotten into you?"

"Do you have any idea how embarrassing this is? The youth director engaged to my mother! Couldn't you have at least asked me how I felt about it?"

"For your information, Jennie, Michael wanted to do just that. He was concerned about your reaction. Unfortunately, you were in Florida. I told him that you were a mature young lady and that you would be able to handle it fine."

"Yeah right, Mom," Jennie said as she scrambled to her feet. "I overreacted. I'll handle it." She'd handle it all right, but Jennie wasn't certain how mature she'd be. When she'd entered the house and was out of earshot she muttered, "I just won't go to any more youth meetings. Maybe I'll find another church or move to another town." Jennie sighed in frustration and decidedly put the matter aside. She didn't have time to worry about Michael . . .

she had to tell Lisa about Rocky and the latest delivery.

Jennie headed for her room to call Lisa. No one answered and Jennie left a message on the machine. She'd try again later, but in the meantime, Jennie intended to check out the florist shop that had delivered the roses to Allison.

She skimmed the Portland Yellow pages . . . no listing under *Tricia's Flowers*. Closing her eyes, she tried to visualize the logo on the side of the van. If she could just recall the address. There had been something different about it, because she remembered wondering why it was coming from so far away. Vancouver. That was it. Not only had it been from another town but from another state. Vancouver was located just over the state line, north of the Columbia River.

That meant the stalker probably lived over there. Jennie had forgotten about that fact when she'd described the van to Mr. Beaumont. She reached for the phone, intending to call him, then stopped. *What if he's involved, McGrady? Wouldn't it be better to do a little investigating on your own first?*

Jennie decided it would and placed another call to Lisa. This time Lisa answered. Jennie quickly filled her in on the van delivering flowers and her run-in with Rocky and Allison's father.

"Rocky said he'd call in the information, so I imagine he told the police, but just in case he and Beaumont are involved, I think we should check out the florist shop ourselves."

Lisa agreed, and five minutes later Jennie climbed back in the car and headed for Lisa's. Jennie was probably way off base, but the family money, Beaumont's political interests, and his sidekick, Rocky, reminded Jennie of a movie she'd seen once where this woman had no idea her father and the man she'd married were mobsters. She found out the hard way. True, it was just a movie, but what if Beaumont and Rocky had ties to some huge crime syndicate, like smuggling drugs, or diamonds, or. . . . *Give it a rest, McGrady.* Jennie brought her overactive imagination to an abrupt halt. *Even if Beaumont was rude, he did seem concerned about Allison.* She'd do well to stop these wild speculations and stick to the facts.

Once they reached Vancouver, Jennie pulled off the freeway at the first exit and found a phone booth at a gas station. "Let's hope Tricia's is on this side of town," Jennie said as she leafed through the yellow pages under florists. "Here it is," she said, poising her pen above a scrap of paper Lisa had dug out of her purse. "We're in luck. It's out by Vancouver Mall."

She and Lisa and their moms had gone shopping there a couple of times, and Jennie knew exactly where to go.

"Great," Lisa said, grinning as she slid into the passenger seat and buckled herself in. "Maybe we can get some shopping in. I still need a new dress for the party."

"Cutting it kind of close, aren't you? The party's tomorrow." Jennie eased out of the parking place.

"I know, but I want it to be just right."

Jennie wanted to laugh, but didn't. Her cousin couldn't look anything but right. Lisa had a way of making even the grungiest clothes look fashionable. "Let me guess—you haven't been able to find a dress to match your new nail polish."

"You don't need to be sarcastic." Lisa pouted. "But you're right. I've looked in practically every dress shop in Portland. I had no idea there were so many different shades of green. You don't mind, do you?"

Jennie didn't. Shopping with Lisa and Aunt Kate was like going to an art gallery. "Okay, but only for an hour. We have to get back. Allison's expecting us for dinner."

The florist shop was in a small shopping center near the mall, and Jennie found a parking space right in front. A bell tinkled as she opened the door. It smelled of flowers and potpourri. A combination of fresh and dried flower arrangements lined the walls and hung from the ceiling. A slender woman stood behind the counter, unwrapping a bundle of dried roses.

8

"Hi." She smiled and set the flowers aside. "I'm Tricia. How can I help you?"

Jennie stepped up to the counter, uncertain as to how to proceed. After a moment's hesitation, she decided on a straightforward approach. "Your van made a delivery to a friend's house today. Allison Beaumont. And we were wondering if you could tell us who sent her the flowers."

Tricia frowned. "Gee, I don't know if I should give out information like that. Client confidentiality, you know."

Jennie nodded. "I can appreciate that, but our friend has been getting some threatening messages. We think whoever is sending these flowers might be a stalker."

"Her life might be in danger," Lisa added.

Tricia glanced from Jennie to Lisa, then shrugged. "Hold on, let me check my file." She turned toward a small computer on a desk behind her and started typing. "That was Beaumont on Lakeview Drive?"

Jennie nodded. Excitement charged through her. *This is going to be a snap, McGrady. You are getting good at this detective stuff.* In a second they'd have the name of Allison's stalker. The case would be solved. Gram would be proud . . . so would Dad.

"Gee, I'm sorry. I don't have a name. He must have paid cash."

"Oh no." Jennie's heart dropped to her shoes; then picking up on what Tricia had said, she added, "You said he. It was a man?"

"I think so. Actually, I'm not sure . . ."

"Please try," Lisa said as she rested her arms on the counter.

"Let me think." The woman tipped her head back and closed her eyes. "Beaumont . . . Beaumont . . . roses . . .

"Yes. I do remember him," Tricia said at last. "Sure didn't seem like the kind of guy who'd hurt anyone, though. Sweet as could be. Tall, about six feet. Longish curly blond hair, blue eyes. And he was wearing a cowboy hat. Reminded me of that country singer—Alan Jackson. About your age, I think. Cute, and kind of shy." She shrugged. "I'm sorry. That's about all I can tell you."

Jennie and Lisa thanked her. "Would you call me if he comes in again?" Jennie asked, jotting her name and number on a note pad on the counter. Tricia agreed.

As they reached the door, Tricia stopped them. "Say," she called, "why are you asking these questions and not the police? You a detective or something?"

"Or something," Jennie smiled. "The police will probably want to question you too. Just as soon as I tell them about this guy."

Tricia nodded. "Well, much as I hate to lose a customer, if he's in to stalking young girls, I hope they catch him."

Once in the car, Jennie took a deep breath. "I have a feeling Rocky might be Allison's stalker. He fits Tricia's description."

"He and about a third of the male population in Portland," Lisa said.

Jennie started the car. "Maybe, but I'll bet anything Rocky's the one. I didn't tell him and Mr. Beaumont about the Vancouver address, but even without that, you'd think the police would have figured it out. I'll bet Rocky never called them."

Jennie headed for the mall, with shopping the farthest thing from her mind. She was planning her next encounter with the mysterious gardener.

Jennie promised to catch up with Lisa in Nordstrom's as soon as she'd made a phone call to the police. She asked for one of the two officers who'd come to the house the evening before and a few seconds later heard Greg Donovan's friendly greeting.

"Hi, Jennie. What can I do for you?" Jennie told him about the phone call she'd had after they'd gone and about the van and her visit to Tricia's Flowers.

"Hey, listen," Greg said. "Much as I appreciate the information, I wish you had let us check out the florist shop. Did it ever occur to you that the owner could be behind this?"

Jennie gulped. It hadn't. "I'm sorry. You're right. I should have called you first."

"Listen, Jennie. I appreciate your help, but I don't want you getting caught in the middle. Stalkers are often unpredictable and relentless—not to mention dangerous." After listening to a stern lecture about letting the police handle the investigation, Jennie said goodbye.

It wasn't until after she'd hung up and had gotten to the escalators that she realized Donovan hadn't answered her question about Rocky. She was beginning to understand why so many of the private detectives she read about had this kind of love-hate relationship with cops. They wanted information but didn't want to share any.

She had to admit, though, Donovan was right about the danger of pursuing a stalker. From now on, she'd leave the investigating to the police—most of it, anyway. Jennie wandered through the racks of clothes until she found Lisa.

"Any luck?" she asked.

"Not finding a green one. But what do you think of this?" Lisa held up a soft cotton dress with a bold floral print.

"Pretty."

"I think so too. There's more green in it than in the others. And, it's on sale."

"Good. Buy it and let's get going."

"What about you? Aren't you getting one?"

"Me? What do I need with another dress? I have two perfectly good ones hanging in my closet. I'll just wear the blue one."

Lisa rolled her eyes. "That's one thing I'll never understand about you, Jen. Don't get me wrong, I like your dresses, but wouldn't you like a little more variety?"

"I can't afford variety. You know that. We're a single-parent family, remember." *But not for long, McGrady. Michael is out to change that.* Ignoring the depressing thought, Jennie said, "Even if we could afford it, clothes just aren't that important to me. As long as I have my jeans and a few tops, I'm happy."

"I know. . . . It's just that I feel guilty, always getting new clothes while you . . ."

"Hey, I'm not complaining, but I will be if you don't hurry up."

Lisa picked out a dozen more dresses, tried them all

on, then decided on the first one. Jennie waited patiently—well, as patiently as she could. One did not push Lisa Calhoun unless one wanted to wait even longer. On the way down the escalator, Lisa spotted a ruffled bow in the same shade of blue silk as the dress Jennie planned to wear to the party.

"This is perfect for you," Lisa crooned as she gathered Jennie's long thick hair and clipped it into the bow.

This, Jennie did buy. Wearing her hair swept up and secured with a bow would be a nice touch—something different.

A couple of hours later Lisa and Jennie arrived at Allison's. Rocky let them in, but before he could greet them, Allison bounced in wearing a pastel pink bikini with a matching crocheted cover-up.

"Where have you been?" Allison demanded. "I thought you were coming this afternoon. It's almost dinnertime."

"Sorry," Jennie muttered. "We were at the mall. Lisa bought a new dress for your party."

Allison gave Lisa an understanding smile and ushered them in. "Let's go upstairs so you can change. I hope you brought your swimsuits. We've still got time for a swim before we eat."

Allison led them to her room and closed the door. White and pastel pink curtains and bedclothes ruffled and poofed out everywhere, reminding Jennie of cotton candy. This was definitely Allison. After making a quick change, Lisa and Jennie followed Allison down the wide spiral staircase, along a long carpeted hallway and through a utility area to the backyard. It looked like something out of *Better Homes and Gardens*.

The Olympic-sized pool sparkled like an aquamarine

gemstone surrounded by tile and tubs of summer flowers. Patio tables complete with padded chairs and umbrellas graced the deck. Nearby, water cascaded from a high stone wall into a Jacuzzi. Lounge chairs and small drink tables had been strategically placed along both sides. Lounging on the nearest one was Paige Matthews. She rose slowly and came forward to greet them, looking like a candidate for the Miss America pageant.

"Hi." A broad grin lit up her face. "It's been forever since I've seen you, Jennie. Love your tan. Lisa told us you'd been to Florida."

Jennie liked Paige's tan too, and her deep red swimsuit and sun-streaked hair, but she didn't say so. Meetings like this made her feel self-conscious and awkward. What Jennie wanted to do was ask her how she felt about Allison these days. Unfortunately, it was too soon to get into details about Allison and Ed Brodie, so she opted for safer ground and asked, "How's your summer going?"

"Wonderful!" Paige held up a perfectly manicured hand to reveal a glistening diamond. "That's how my summer is going. Eddie has asked me to marry him. Isn't that great?"

"Wow." Lisa gasped. "It's beautiful. When did this happen?"

"Last night," Paige answered with a sigh. "It was so romantic. We're going to be married right after graduation."

Allison draped an arm over Paige's shoulder. "She's asked me to be a bridesmaid. I'm so excited."

"Aren't you a little young?" Jennie blurted. As soon as the words left her mouth, she regretted it. *Nice going, McGrady. Just spit out whatever comes to your mind.*

Paige flushed, then laughed, drawing her hand back.

"Not really," she said defensively. "I'm almost seventeen. My mother got married when she was sixteen."

Jennie shrugged. Marriage wasn't on her list of things to talk about at the moment—what with Mom's engagement to Michael—so she tried to change the subject. "Where's B.J.?" she asked, noting that Allison's new sister hadn't joined them.

"Mom took her shopping. She finally agreed to let Mom and Dad buy her some things—I can't believe how stubborn she's been about it. She says she hates her room, which is totally rude. Mom and I spent days decorating it. And you'd think she actually liked those rags she's been wearing. Mom says she's resisting change and to give her time. The clothes and a couple of rings are all she has left of her old life with our real mother."

Jennie frowned, understanding in part what B.J. must be feeling. "It would be hard to go from being poor to being rich. Not to mention losing her mom. . . ." Then thinking about her own box of Dad's things, added, "Holding on to the stuff her mom bought probably helps her deal with the loss." Once again the conversation had drifted too close to home and Jennie was glad for Lisa's suggestion that they head for the pool.

After splashing around and playing catch for half an hour, the other girls announced they were going in to change. "I'll be up in a few minutes," Jennie said. "After I swim a few laps." Jennie swam the length of the pool about six times, then hauled herself out of the water and reclined in the sun on one of the lounge chairs to catch her breath. She closed her eyes and waited until her breathing returned to normal. *You're getting out of shape, McGrady*, she scolded. It had been too long since she'd worked out.

"Nice stroke," a low, male voice remarked.

Jennie jumped to her feet and nearly collided with Rocky. The gardener, or whatever he was, reached out a hand to steady her. "Sorry, I didn't mean to frighten you. I was just admiring your style. You in competition or anything?"

His wide grin and easy stance unnerved her. Or maybe it was the fact he could be the stalker. Jennie stepped back and grabbed for her towel. "Ah . . . no . . . unless you count the swim team at school."

Rocky nodded. "I haven't seen you around here before today. You known Allison long?"

Something about the way he'd asked told Jennie this wasn't a casual conversation. Did he still suspect her? Or maybe he was aiming to make Jennie one of his victims as well. "We go to school together," she answered.

"Just wondered," he said as he lowered himself onto one of the deck chairs beside hers. "Hope you don't mind. I was taking a break and decided to sit out here for a while. It's peaceful . . . don't you think?"

"Yeah." *At least it was before you came*. The last part she kept to herself. "Well, I'd better get back inside with the others."

"So soon?" Rocky asked. "I was hoping maybe you'd stay and talk to me for a few minutes."

Jennie shrugged, trying not to reveal her suspicions about him. She sat on the lounge chair again. Why not. This was a great opportunity to find out more about the number one suspect on her list—next, of course, to B.J. The thought struck her that Rocky and B.J. might be working together—after all, they certainly had opportunity. "Sure." Jennie hesitated, then said, "I guess—"

"I wanted—" he said at the same time, then laughed.

67

His blue eyes sparkled and Jennie looked away. "I just wanted to apologize for this afternoon. I hope I didn't come on too strong. It's just that when I saw you there with those flowers . . . well, with all that's been going on and you not having been around, I thought . . ."

"It's okay. I'm sorry too. I shouldn't have picked them up. It was dumb of me." Jennie twisted her braid around her finger. "So what did the police say?" Jennie asked, even though she suspected he hadn't called.

Rocky shrugged. "Not much. A love note and a bunch of roses can hardly be considered threatening. As far as I know, they weren't able to track down the lead."

Probably because you didn't give them one, Jennie felt like saying. For a moment she considered telling Rocky about the Vancouver address, then decided not to. The less he knew about her involvement in the case, the better.

Rocky paused to pull off his blue cotton shirt, then stretched out on the lounge next to Jennie. "Think I'll catch some rays," he said, winking. "It's been a long day."

Jennie couldn't help noticing his muscular chest. No doubt about it. The guy was a hunk. *He may be gorgeous,* her inner voice warned, *but he could be dangerous.* She glanced at him again, trying not to stare. *And you have to admit, McGrady, he's the cleanest gardener you've ever seen.*

The more Jennie thought about it, the more she was convinced that Rocky was not who he seemed. She made a mental note to ask Allison about him. In the meantime, she had a few questions herself. "The grounds here are beautiful," Jennie commented. "Must be a full-time job to keep them up. Do you do it alone?"

Rocky shaded his eyes with his hand and peered at her. He opened his mouth to answer when a piercing scream from inside the house brought both of them to their feet.

9

Rocky reached Allison's room only seconds before Jennie. Allison, nearly as pale as her swimsuit, clutched a towel to her chest with one hand and clung to Lisa's arm with the other. Lisa guided the girl to the nearest chair and lowered her into it. Paige and Lisa looked nearly as shaken as Allison.

"What's wrong? What happened?" Jennie and Rocky asked together.

Lisa pointed toward the bathroom.

Jennie ran toward the door. Rocky put out an arm to stop her. "Wait here," he ordered as he slipped through the open door and looked around.

Jennie glanced back at Lisa. "What's going on?"

"The mirror," Lisa squeaked. Her voice reflected the fear in her eyes.

Ignoring Rocky's orders, Jennie entered the bathroom. On the large vanity mirror above the sink someone had drawn a crude picture of a rose and written a message in red:

I'M GETTING CLOSER
PRINCESS DIE !!!

The last two words had been smudged. "She tried to wipe it off," Lisa said, coming up behind Jennie. "Paige and I pulled her away. I thought the police would want to see it."

Jennie nodded, staring at the mirror as the implications settled in on her. The stalker had been here—in this room. Rocky ushered Jennie and Lisa out of the bathroom just as Mr. and Mrs. Beaumont rushed into the room. Whatever had been holding Allison together until then crumbled. The girls took turns telling what they knew, which wasn't much. The mirror had been clean when Lisa and Jennie had used the bathroom earlier to change. Allison, when she'd calmed down enough to talk, verified that there had been nothing on it when they'd gone downstairs to swim.

While the girls were in the pool, someone had gone into the house, sneaked upstairs to Allison's room, written the message, and gotten away without anyone seeing them.

If Rocky had been on the job, Jennie reasoned, it wouldn't have happened. Unless maybe he had done it. Of course, it could have been B.J.

Mr. Beaumont must have been thinking the same thing because the moment Jennie's mind formed the name, he yelled, "Where's B.J.?"

"I'm right here," she said, pushing off from the wall.

Jennie wondered how long she'd been there. And more importantly, how long had she been home?

"Do you know anything about this?" The harsh tone of his voice made the question sound like an accusation.

For an instant, Jennie thought she'd recognized a glint of hurt in B.J.'s eyes, but when she looked again, she saw nothing but hate.

When B.J. didn't answer, Mr. Beaumont clenched his fist and asked again. "Well, do you?"

"I don't know why you even bothered to ask. You already think I did it." She turned and walked to the door, then spun around and glared at her father. "If you're so sure it was me, why don't you have me arrested." B.J. disappeared down the hall, but her words hung on the now-stale air. A door slammed and the windows rattled.

For a moment Jennie thought Mr. Beaumont would explode, then suddenly, like an actor changing scenes, he cleared his throat and began giving orders. Mrs. Beaumont was to take Allison to the "master suite" to rest. He sent Rocky downstairs to his office where they would "discuss the matter" after he'd talked to B.J.

Turning to Jennie, Lisa, and Paige, Mr. Beaumont ran a hand through his hair and cleared his throat. "I'm sorry you girls had to see this. You're welcome to stay, of course . . ."

"I—I think I'd like to go home." Paige shifted from one foot to the other. Her tiny features were drawn and pale, reminding Jennie of a frightened bird. "Tell Allie I'll be back in the morning," she said as she backed out of the room.

Mr. Beaumont nodded and lifted his gaze to Jennie and Lisa. "We'll stay," Jennie said. "Allison might need us later." Nothing short of dynamite could dislodge Jennie now. This was getting much too interesting, and she had too many unanswered questions.

Jennie couldn't tell how Mr. Beaumont felt about their staying. He silently ushered them out of Allison's room to a large guest room across the hall. "It would be best if everyone stays out of here for now," he said, closing Allison's door.

"Maybe we should go too," Lisa said as she paced across the guest room's plush white carpet. "This is all too weird. I'm sorry I got you into this."

"Don't be. I'm not giving up until I find out what's going on around here." Jennie rummaged through her overnight bag.

"What are you doing?" Lisa asked as she came up behind Jennie.

"Looking for something to make some notes on." Jennie fished around and finally came up with a small spiral note pad. "Okay." Jennie settled on the bed. Excitement coursed through her. "Let's see what we've got so far."

Lisa dropped onto a chair and recounted some of the details of the case. Within a few minutes Jennie had listed the various floral deliveries and threatening phone calls she and Lisa knew about. Then she entered the information she had about the man with a gun from the night before and the call to Jennie's house. At the bottom she wrote, "message on mirror—red lipstick." Jennie scooted off the bed. "C'mon."

"Where to?"

"Allison's bathroom. I want to have another look. Maybe we can find some clues."

"No!" Lisa spread herself across the door, blocking Jennie's way. "We can't. It's too awful. Jennie, I can't go back in there."

Jennie nodded in understanding. "Okay. Wait here for me."

Lisa started to object, then, as if reading the determination in her cousin's eyes, stepped aside. "All right, but I'm coming too. No way am I staying in here alone." They crept out of the guest room and down the hall to Allison's bedroom. Jennie turned the knob and eased open the door. The room looked as perfect as when she and Lisa had first arrived. Despite the open window, a strong scent of cleaning solution assaulted their nostrils. "This is strange," Jennie whispered. "Looks like someone's been in here and cleaned."

Jennie knew even before she opened the bathroom door what she'd find. Nothing. Someone had wiped away every shred of evidence. "The police aren't going to like this," Jennie said, then realized with a start they'd probably never been called.

"I'm scared, Jennie." Lisa tugged at Jennie's shirt sleeve. "Let's get out of here."

"I can't go yet. Something really strange is going on here, and I intend to find out what. Besides, even if the Beaumonts aren't calling the cops, I am. I want to make sure I can give them a detailed report."

"You're right. We can't give up now. Allison needs our help more than ever."

Using a washcloth so as not to leave any fingerprints, Jennie opened each drawer and searched through them.

"What are you looking for?" Lisa asked.

"The lipstick. I was hoping maybe whoever did it might have left it behind. It could be an important clue." Jennie rummaged through what looked like Allison's makeup drawer. She found about a dozen tubes of lipstick, all in various shades of pink. Jennie closed the last drawer, then picked up the wastebasket. She ruffled through the trash and at the bottom found what she'd been looking for. "Hand me those tweezers," Jennie said, pointing to an open drawer.

"Why?"

"There might be prints on it. I wonder where the cap is."

Lisa cringed when Jennie held up the shiny gold tube with its brilliant red lipstick worn down to the nub. "You think that's the stuff he used?"

Jennie shrugged. "Allison ever use red lipstick?"

"Not that I recall." Lisa wandered over to the open window and rubbed her arms.

"What about Paige?"

"Yeah, she does sometimes." Lisa nodded in the direction of the pool. They watched as B.J. climbed out of the pool, stretched out on a lounge chair, picked up a book, and began to read.

"Doesn't seem to be broken up about it, does she?" Jennie asked.

"Do you think B.J. wrote the message?" Lisa asked.

"I don't know." Before the incident with B.J. and her dad, Jennie would have bet on it, but something in her face—confusion, hurt—made Jennie question her original suspicions. "It's too early to tell." Tucking the lipstick into a plastic bag she found in one of the drawers, Jennie stepped away from the window and made another note on her pad regarding the cleanup and the red lipstick.

As she read over the notes again, she stopped with the notation about the gunman of the night before.

"Lisa," she mused, as she tapped the end of the pen against her lips, "do you think you can remember where Mr. B.'s gun case is? I think we ought to check it out."

Lisa led the way back to the main living area. "The gun collection is downstairs." After opening two closets and a pantry, they found the stairs and followed them to the lower part of the house and into a long dark hallway.

"Where's a light switch?" Jennie asked in a whisper as she felt along the wall.

"I don't know. There should be a bathroom . . .

here." Light flooded the small room, giving them enough light to find the switches in the other rooms.

After going past an exercise room, a room that looked like a miniature movie theater, and a large storage closet, they found the den.

"This is it," Lisa whispered as she opened the door.

Jennie stepped in. The hairs on the back of her neck snapped to attention. Several pairs of eyes peered out of the darkness. A large form loomed off to her right. "There's someone—or something in here," she yelped.

Lisa stepped up beside her and turned on the light. "Don't worry," she reassured. "They're stuffed."

In the light, the form Jennie had seen turned out to be a black bear standing on its hind legs, ready to attack. Jennie's gaze wandered over the room. It looked like a hunter's trophy room—an elk head held a prominent position over the fireplace; a deer, a cougar, and a couple of fish that had to be six feet long nearly covered the walls. In addition to the bear, Jennie noticed a couple of pheasants, a coyote, and several other small animals she couldn't name.

Jennie whispered, "He's got more animals in here than the zoo."

"Allison said he used to hunt a lot."

Beaumont's den had a forest green carpet with rich dark mahogany wood. "I wish Dad could see this." As soon as the words slipped out, her memory kicked in. *He's gone, McGrady.* Tears stung her eyes and Jennie quickly wiped them away. She glanced at Lisa.

"He would love it." Lisa gave her a knowing smile and hooked her arm through Jennie's. "Come on. The gun collection is over here."

A combination book and gun case lined an entire wall

of the den. With one swift pass, Jennie found what she was looking for. A metal plate beneath the indentation that once housed a gun read *1880 Colt Lightning— Pinkerton Detective Agency*.

"You think this is the same gun the guy had the other night?" Lisa asked.

"I'm sure of it. But why? Why steal an old gun like this when it's so easy to buy them on the street?"

"Then again," Lisa said, "why buy a gun when you've got a whole case of them right here?"

Jennie tried to undo the latch holding the doors. "Locked. Whoever took the gun either has a key or had easy access to it. This is beginning to look more and more like an inside job."

"B.J.?"

"Or Rocky, or Mr. Beaumont." Jennie pulled the note pad and pen out of her back pocket. "Or maybe Allison herself."

"Not Allison," Lisa said, shaking her head. "Don't forget, I walked upstairs with her. Paige and I were there when she found the message."

"Yes, but while we were swimming she did go inside for a few minutes to use the bathroom."

"That's true, but so did Paige and I."

Jennie wrinkled her nose. "We're not getting very far. We're missing something. I just can't think what."

Jennie entered the information about the missing gun on her note pad. "We'd better get back upstairs before someone notices we're gone." Jennie turned to go just as the lights went out and the door clicked shut.

10

"M-maybe it was the wind," Lisa stammered.

"Shh . . ." Jennie put her ear to the door. "Footsteps." She glanced at Lisa. "Definitely not the wind."

Jennie switched on the light and pulled on the doorknob. When it wouldn't budge, panic edged in. She gasped, remembering the fire . . . she and Sarah trapped in that cabin . . . *Easy, McGrady, pull yourself together. There's no fire . . . this isn't Florida.*

"Jennie, what is it, what's wrong?"

"I . . . nothing." Jennie looked at the large wooden door. "I'm just trying to find a way out of here." She tried to imagine herself taking a running jump, lying flat out and hitting the door with both feet, then quickly dismissed the idea. That was more Gram's speed. Jennie hadn't taken a karate lesson in her life.

She glanced over at the gun case. If she had to, she could break the glass, take out a gun, and shoot the door lock. But she wouldn't—not yet. The thought of having a way out eased her mind.

"We could call the police," Jennie suggested, then quickly shoved that idea aside as well. This wouldn't be a good time. If they called the cops now, she and Lisa would probably be arrested for breaking and entering.

77

"We could beat on the door and call for help," Lisa said as she tried the knob again, then raised her fists.

"Wait. I have an idea." Jennie went back to Mr. Beaumont's desk, checked the phone, and opened the drawers.

"Jennie, you shouldn't . . ."

Ignoring her cousin's protests Jennie continued her search for a phone book. "They have three lines. This one must be Mr. Beaumont's, but which is Allison's?" She looked up at Lisa. "Do you remember Allison's phone number?"

One of the lights on the telephone flashed, and on impulse Jennie picked it up. When no one else answered, she said hello.

"Hi . . . um . . . Allison?" The voice sounded out of breath, or like the guy might be nervous.

"Who is this?" Jennie asked, softening her voice so she'd sound more like Allison.

"Did you get the flowers?"

Jennie almost dropped the phone. She put her hand over the mouthpiece and whispered to Lisa, "It's him . . . it's the stalker."

Stay calm, McGrady . . . keep him talking. She took a deep breath to slow her racing heart and said, "Y-yes."

"Good." After a long pause, the voice said, "I thought I'd come by later tonight so we could talk."

"Here?" Jennie could hardly think over the boom-boom of her pulse pounding in her ears. This was too weird. It didn't make sense. Still, neither did stalking people. Her first impulse was to say no. *This is your big break, McGrady. You can catch him red-handed.* "Sure . . ." she stammered, "that'll be fine."

"Good. See you around ten."

"Who is this?" she asked. But the line had gone dead.

Jennie returned the phone to its cradle and told Lisa what the caller had said.

"That's perfect. We'll tell Allison and set a trap for him. We'll call the police and they'll nab him and it will be all over. . . . Jennie, what's wrong?"

Jennie stroked her chin and lowered herself into Mr. B.'s soft green leather chair. "That voice . . . I've heard it before, but it didn't sound the same as the guy the other night. . . ."

"Maybe he disguised his voice," Lisa said, leaning against the desk.

"Maybe, but something about this doesn't feel right." Jennie set the nagging feeling aside. She'd deal with it later; right now, she had to get them out of Beaumont's den. Jennie punched the number she'd just been on. Allison answered on the third ring, saying she'd just gotten back to her room.

Leaving out the part about the caller, Jennie told her what had happened and within three minutes, the door opened and Allison appeared. She looked like she'd been on a week-long crying binge. "I'm so sorry this happened. Who would lock you in here?" Allison grabbed at her throat and leaned against the wall. "He's in the house. He's . . ."

Jennie thought for a moment Allison was going to lose it again. She put her arms around Allison's shoulder. "I don't think so. If he was here, I'm sure he's gone now, unless . . ." *Unless the stalker is Rocky or B.J., or even your father.* Jennie didn't say the last part out loud. No sense in upsetting her any more—at least not right now.

"Never mind," Jennie finished. "Let's get out of here before your dad catches us in here."

"Good idea," Lisa said, guiding them out and closing the door. "I know it sounds terrible with so many more important things going on, but do you think we could eat dinner? I'm starved."

The detour to food and hostessing mobilized Allison to action. She glanced at her watch. "Oh . . . of course, it's almost seven. That's a great idea. Let's order a pizza. We'll send Rocky over to *Antonio's*."

The girls went back upstairs and spent the next few minutes putting together an order. Rocky shifted impatiently as Allison specified their pizza toppings. He clearly did not want to go, and Jennie couldn't help but wonder why. After all, he was supposed to be working for the Beaumonts.

Jennie, Lisa, Allison, and a disgruntled B.J., whom they'd found sulking in her room, took the pizza and drinks to the pool area. For the next half hour they gorged themselves. Detective work—or maybe it was being scared out of your wits—sure gave you an appetite. The four of them managed to put away a large pan pizza supreme and two pitchers of diet cola.

Reluctant to talk about the stalker, they kept the conversation on a safe level and discussed the party instead. At least Lisa and Allison did. B.J., strangely silent, stared at some spot on the other side of the pool. Was she involved in all this . . . and if so, to what extent? Had B.J. written the message on the mirror? Had she locked them in her dad's office? Did she know the guy was coming over? That might account for her behavior.

Soon Jennie would have to broach the subject of the stalker's visit. She'd wait as long as she could, but sooner or later, Allison would need to know about her guest. Jennie glanced at her watch. Eight-thirty. But not yet. In half an hour, she promised herself.

Jennie leaned back in her chair and closed her eyes. The trouble with mysteries was that there were always so many angles . . . so many questions.

Who would want to stalk Allison? Why would some-one steal a gun from Beaumont's gun case? Why stalk Allison? Why send love notes one time and threats the next? Why write a message on Allison's mirror? Why lock her and Lisa into Beaumont's den? And why would the stalker call to announce his arrival as if he were setting up a date? It didn't make sense.

Jennie opened her eyes and caught B.J. staring at her. The girl quickly looked away then jumped to her feet. The chair she'd been sitting in clattered to the concrete floor. She stooped to pick it up. "Look . . ." she began. "I—I have something to tell you. I . . ."

Jennie leaned forward.

"Not here," B.J. said. "Al's room."

They silently took the remains of their dinner into the kitchen and headed upstairs. Once inside the cotton candy room, B.J. closed the door and leaned against it. "I'm the one who locked you in the den." B.J. dropped into the chair nearest the door. As though reading the question in Jennie's mind, she added, "But I didn't write that message, I swear it. I guess I was just upset that everyone suspects me."

Jennie opened her mouth to deny the accusation, but B.J. cut her off. "Don't bother denying it . . . I can see it in your eyes. Anyway, when I came in from the pool I heard you downstairs and . . . I don't know . . . I guess I just wanted to scare you or something. I'm sorry."

"I never suspected you." Allison came up behind B.J. and put a hand on her shoulder.

"Thanks." B.J. hunched her shoulders forward. "Anyway, I think I know who the stalker is."

All talk about the den was forgotten. "Who?" the girls asked together.

B.J. straightened. Her arrogant look had returned. Jennie half expected her to say, "That's for me to know and you to find out," or "You're the detective, you tell me." But she didn't. She glanced at the door and whispered, "Rocky."

Jennie let out a long breath. She'd suspected him herself, until the phone call in the den. Now it didn't seem likely—unless the call was just another ploy to scare Allison and he had no intention of showing up. "Do you have proof?" she asked.

"No—not exactly. It's just that I've been watching him. Dad hired him a couple of days after I came. There's something weird about him. He's no gardener, that's for sure. He's always snooping around."

"That's true," Allison said. "I catch him looking at me all the time. Part of the problem is that Dad asked him to keep an eye on me. I don't mind when we're out running around, but it certainly isn't necessary in the house." Allison drew in a ragged breath. "He gives me the creeps."

"Have you told your folks?" Lisa asked.

Allison nodded. "Daddy just told me I was imagining things and that Rocky came highly recommended."

Jennie dropped into a white wicker chair with a pink pad. *Recommended by whom?* "Not that I don't trust your dad, Allison, but I'd sure like to know more about Rocky. Do you think we could find out where he lived before he moved in here?"

Allison frowned. "Dad would probably have records in his computer—or in the file cabinet in his office, but there's no way . . ."

"Well, never mind," Jennie said, an idea forming in the back of her mind. "Maybe between us, we can ask the right questions. In fact . . ." Jennie turned to Lisa. "You'd be perfect. He hasn't really met you yet. Why don't you get him alone and ask him about his past?"

"O-o-oh." Lisa grinned. "Undercover work. I like that." She turned her back and looked over her right shoulder, giving the others a sultry pout. "How's this? Think he'll be so swayed by my charms he'll tell me everything?"

Jennie laughed. "He'll probably run the other way. Just act natural."

"Look," Allison called from the window. "There he is now—cleaning the pool."

Jennie and B.J. hurried to the window and looked over Allison's shoulder. "Perfect. Okay, Lisa, this is it. Go on down there and pretend you're interested."

Lisa joined them at the window and peered into the garden below. "That won't be hard. He's really cute." She ran out of the room and returned only seconds later with her emerald swimsuit and headed for Allison's bathroom. She stopped in the doorway. "Ah . . . Jennie . . . what about . . . you know."

"Go ahead and get your suit on. I'll tell them."

"Tell us what?" B.J. asked.

Jennie told them about the phone call she'd taken earlier. "Like I said, Rocky could be involved somehow; it didn't sound like him, but who knows. He could be disguising his voice to throw us off."

Lisa came out of the bathroom and headed for the door. "I'm ready . . . I guess." She sounded reluctant and Jennie didn't blame her.

"You don't have to do this," Jennie said.

"I know, but you're right. I'm the only one he doesn't really know. Besides, you'll be here—won't you?"

"He won't try anything with a house full of people," B.J. assured.

Jennie gave Lisa the same assurance, but as she stood at the window with the others, she offered up a prayer just in case.

11

For the next twenty minutes they watched an animated discussion between Rocky and Lisa. Lisa laughed, flirted, talked, and listened as Rocky—Jennie hoped—told her his life story.

At nine-fifteen, Lisa and Rocky both stood. She turned away from him and headed into the house. He watched her go.

"He's definitely interested," B.J. said.

"The jerk," Jennie muttered.

"I should tell Daddy," Allison said. "Maybe if he knew Rocky was flirting with one of my friends he'd fire him."

Lisa bounced in, her eyes bright with excitement. "I did it. His real name is Robert. He's from Vancouver. He's twenty, single, and . . ." Lisa paused and sighed. "If I were allowed to date older guys I would definitely be interested."

"Lisa," she scolded, "you sound like you want to go out with him. He's a suspect, remember?"

"I know . . . but he's just so sweet, you know. I don't think he's the one. He doesn't seem like the criminal type to me." Lisa's smile vanished. "I botched it, didn't I? You sent me out to get information and I come back with a hunk report."

"You did great," Allison soothed. "Probably better than any of us could have."

"Right," Jennie said. "We've got enough to do a background check—providing he told you the truth. Did he tell you his last name?"

"Kennedy. Robert . . . Kennedy." Lisa's voice trailed off as she realized the joke was on her. She winced. "Oh, no . . . wait'll I get my hands on him . . ."

"We've been had." B.J. made a fist and socked the bed. "Do you think he knows we suspect him?"

A sour feeling started at the pit of Jennie's stomach. She didn't want to think about the implications. "He might," Jennie said, "but I don't think he'll do anything as long as we stick together. We'll keep an eye on him for now." Later, Jennie decided, when everyone was asleep, she'd have a look in Beaumont's office and see what she could dig up. She thought about telling the others what she had in mind, then decided against it. Might be better to handle this one alone. In the meantime, they had another urgent matter to deal with.

"It's past nine," Jennie said. "We should decide how we're going to handle Allison's visitor. He said he'd be by around ten." The girls decided to wait on the patio off the guest room on the second floor where Lisa and Jennie were staying. Wisteria wove through the wood slats making a perfect privacy screen, allowing them to see anyone approaching the house. They'd no sooner gotten settled when they heard a motor and saw headlights turning into the driveway.

"Do you think it's him?" Allison had turned almost chalky white again.

"You can relax, Al." B.J. leaned out over the balcony. "It's Paige . . . and Ed."

Allison joined her sister at the railing. "Hi! We'll be right down."

"No, don't bother," Paige said. "We just had to come by and make sure you were okay, Allison. I—I'm sorry I didn't stay . . . I just couldn't . . ."

"It's okay." Allison leaned over the railing. "I understand. Are you staying over?"

"Ah . . . no. We rented a movie. I'll be over in the morning."

"Hey, Allison!" Ed popped up through the sun roof of Paige's yellow VW. "Paige told me what happened. Cops have any idea who did it?"

"No," Allison said, "but I'm sure they'll find him."

"Hope so, for your sake. Hey, if there's anything I can do, call me. See ya tomorrow." He popped back inside and leaned toward Paige.

Paige gunned the motor, practically obliterating their goodbyes. They waved as they tore down the driveway, over the traffic bump, and bounced into the street. Jennie watched their taillights disappear, then turned back to the others.

"I can't see what Paige sees in him," B.J. muttered. "He thinks he's God's gift to women."

"Eddie's not bad," Allison defended.

B.J. snorted. "Right. His ego's bigger than his brain. Besides, any guy who would make a hit on his girl's best friend is pond scum."

"You have to admit, he is kind of cute," Lisa added as she moved from the railing and sank onto one of the patio chairs. "All that dark, thick, curly hair and those gorgeous brown eyes. I could name a dozen girls right now who are dying to go out with him. I hear he kisses like a dream." Lisa sighed. "If I wasn't going with Brad

I'd be tempted to date him myself."

"Don't get your hopes up," Allison warned. "He and Paige are engaged, remember."

"I'd have to side with B.J. on this one." Jennie leaned back against the railing and rested her elbows on the ledge. "I bet I could name a dozen girls he's dumped who'd like to . . ." An approaching car cut her off. Jennie whipped around. She'd have recognized the old Ford truck anywhere. "Hey, that's Jerry Shepherd. What's he doing here?"

Jerry, originally from Texas, lived in Battleground, just north of Vancouver. Jennie stared openmouthed as Jerry parked in the driveway and rang the doorbell. "Hi," he said to whoever answered the door. "Is Allison in?"

That voice. He'd been the one on the phone earlier . . . Jennie was sure of it—well, almost sure. There were a lot of people with southern accents.

"Well, well, well," B.J. said, mimicking his drawl. "Looks like we got us a stalker."

"Don't be ridiculous." Allison laughed nervously. "Jerry wouldn't hurt a fly." She went to the railing and waved. "Jerry, come on in . . . we'll be right down."

Lisa seconded Allison's assertion. "Jerry's president of our youth group at church. We've been friends for years."

"Yeah, well what's he doing here now?" B.J. held up her watch. "It's exactly ten p.m."

Jennie was wondering the same thing. *You're imagining things, McGrady. Jerry would no more stalk Allison Beaumont than rob a bank. He's the nicest guy, next to Ryan, that you know. He's your friend, for Pete's sake.*

He's also tall, with blond curly hair and blue eyes and a cowboy hat. He fits Tricia's description. Before joining the others, Jennie scanned the grounds. She'd called the police earlier and reported the strange phone call.

Apparently they hadn't paid much attention, for she saw no sign of them. Rocky had just finished watering the front lawn and was heading back into the house. He stopped and glanced around as well. As if sensing her presence, he looked up. Their gazes locked. Jennie felt an odd sensation in the pit of her stomach. Dread, foreboding, fear? She swallowed back whatever it was and stepped inside, then hurried downstairs to catch up with the others.

Jerry stood as they entered the living room. He'd taken off his black cowboy hat and was shifting it from one hand to the other. He ran a hand though his hair and stepped toward them. "Jennie, Lisa . . . Allison," he said their names slowly, nodding his head at each of them as he shook their hands. "And you must be Bethany. Heard a lot about you."

"I'll just bet," B.J. mumbled.

"Have a seat." Allison took his hand and led him into the large family room. Once they were all seated he lowered his lanky frame onto the arm of the sofa. "Ah . . . sorry to be callin' so late," he drawled. "But I wanted to talk to y'all before the weekend."

When no one responded, he cleared his throat. "Um . . . today is the last day to register for the overnight hiking trip on the Lewis River. We leave early Saturday morning. None of you had registered so I thought I'd come over and remind you."

Jennie groaned in relief. "That's why you came? Then it wasn't . . ." She'd started to ask about the phone call and the flowers and realized how ridiculous she'd sound. "I'd forgotten all about it." She'd planned on going, but with Michael taking over as youth director, she'd decided not to.

"I went ahead and wrote your name in, Jennie. Michael told me you were going."

Jennie clenched her teeth together so hard she thought her jaw might break. She wanted to scream. *How dare he try to run her life?* Jennie didn't argue. This wasn't the time. She'd deal with Michael later. "Well, then," Jennie said, hoping she sounded normal, "I guess that's settled."

"I'm going," Lisa said. "Brad will, if he doesn't have to work. My folks too—Michael asked them if they'd come along as chaperons." She wrinkled her nose. "It's going to seem more like a family picnic than a youth retreat. Allison, why don't you and B.J come? You'll have fun and it would take your mind off . . . you know."

"Oh, why not," Allison said. "Count me in. With all that's been going on, I wasn't sure I'd go, but maybe a camp-out would be relaxing . . ." Allison smiled at Jerry, and Jennie could almost feel the sparks between them. Jerry and Allison? No way. The cowboy and the princess. Jennie tried not to smile as she imagined the two of them together. Denim and lace. . . . It worked with clothes, maybe it could work for people as well.

Nah. Jerry wasn't Allison's type—he lived on a farm with five brothers and sisters. The family didn't have much money. Even if he liked her, she probably wouldn't. . . . Jennie tried to stop the path her thoughts had taken, but they plowed through her like a runaway train. Jerry knew about guns . . . he'd talked about going hunting with his dad. *You have to admit it, McGrady, if he's interested and she's not, you've got motive.*

Her mind shifted back to the phone call she'd intercepted. Had it been Jerry? Jennie tried to replay the voice in her head. Yes. No. She couldn't be sure. Tomorrow she'd call Tricia again—maybe take a picture of Jerry along. As much as the idea disturbed her, she had to know.

When she tuned back in to the conversation, Allison and Jerry were trying to talk B.J. into going. "You'll have a great time," Jerry promised. "The Lewis River is fantastic. We'll be going by some great waterfalls."

"That part sounds okay," B.J. admitted. "I just don't want anybody trying to shove their religious ideas down my throat."

"We don't do that," Jerry assured. He leaned forward and rested his elbows on his knees, still turning his hat. "I can't promise we won't talk about God—we want everyone to know about Jesus. In the evening we'll have a Bible study around the campfire. We usually get into some serious discussions about religion and politics. Sometimes kids give their testimonies—you know, talk about how God has helped them. But you don't even have to go to that if you don't want to. Mostly, we're just out there to have a good time."

"He's right, B.J.," Lisa said. "Our retreats and camp-outs are a lot of fun. You'll love it."

B.J. finally agreed to go. While Lisa and Allison listened intently to Jerry's instructions on what to bring, B.J. leaned toward Jennie and whispered, "This will give us a chance to keep an eye on this bird."

"He's not the stalker," Jennie whispered back, then pretended to be absorbed in what Jerry was saying. *You've been wrong about people before, McGrady,* a voice in her head persisted. On one hand Jennie couldn't believe that Jerry had anything to do with the terrible threats. On the other, she knew from experience that people were not always what they seemed. Did Jerry have a dark side that drove him to the insidious behavior of a stalker?

Jerry had no sooner hopped into his truck when two police cars with sirens blaring pulled up behind him. Two officers jumped out of the first car, while three others appeared from their hiding places behind the house and shrubs. All had drawn their guns. Jennie hadn't even known they were there.

"You in the truck! Come out with your hands up," a voice boomed.

Jennie watched transfixed as Jerry emerged from the cab with his hands raised. "What's goin' on?"

An officer whipped him around and slammed him up against the cab. His hat fell to the ground. Jennie clamped a hand over her mouth to keep from screaming. She felt like she'd been slugged in the stomach.

"No!" Allison screamed at the officers who'd now frisked and handcuffed him. "Wait! You're making a mistake. Jerry, I'm so sorry!"

Allison and Jennie raced toward the truck. Mr. Beaumont and Rocky stopped them.

"Daddy," Allison pleaded as she grabbed his arm. "They've made a terrible mistake. Jerry didn't do anything."

"What's going on here? Why are you holding this young man?" Mr. Beaumont shouted.

Greg Donovan and an officer Jennie didn't recognize stepped toward them.

"Daddy, please." Allison was near tears now. "Make them let him go."

Beaumont cleared his throat. "Why don't we go inside and see if we can clear this thing up."

"I'm afraid we can't do that, sir," Donovan said. "We have reason to believe this young man has been stalking your daughter."

12

Jennie made the mistake of meeting Jerry's eyes. They were full of questions and hurt. *You set him up, McGrady. He didn't have a chance.* Donovan put him in the back of their squad car, then turned to talk to Jennie. "Thanks for the tip. I'll be out in the morning to give you a report and get your statements." Donovan smiled and ducked into the car.

When the police had gone, Mr. Beaumont headed for the house with Allison still hanging on his arm, pleading with him to do something. Rocky followed mutely behind. Jennie scrunched down and retrieved Jerry's hat, brushed off the dirt, and tried to reshape it. It faded in a blur of tears and Jennie brushed them away.

"Why are you crying?" B.J. asked.

Jennie shrugged. "I'm not sure. It's the hat—they stepped all over it—acted like they didn't even know it was there."

"So what? It's just a hat."

"Not just a hat," Lisa answered softly. "Jerry's dad gave it to him for Christmas last year. He's worn it ever since."

"Like I said, so what?"

Jennie lifted her gaze to meet B.J.'s. "Jerry's dad had

cancer. He died on Christmas Day."

"Oh." B.J.'s eyes softened with understanding. "I guess we'd better get it back to him."

Long after the others had gone to bed Jennie sat in a lounge chair and stared into the dark pool. Tears filled her eyes for the hundredth time, and for the hundredth time she wiped them away.

She sensed a presence before she heard his voice.

"It's kind of late for a swim." Rocky hunkered down beside her and offered her a box of tissues. "Want to talk about it?"

Jennie didn't know if it was the moonlight, or the numbness, but all of a sudden it didn't matter that Rocky had been one of her main suspects or that she barely knew him. His voice was soft and low and Jennie needed to tell someone.

"I betrayed him," she murmured. "Jerry is my friend and I set him up. I never should have called the police."

Rocky moved into the chair beside her. "Why did you?" he asked, his voice still gentle.

"I had too. The call might have been from the real stalker. He might have intended to hurt Allison."

"So you did the right thing."

"I guess, but then why does it seem so wrong?" Not really expecting an answer, Jennie leaned her head back and closed her eyes. "All I see is Jerry looking at me. He didn't even know what was happening. He didn't have a clue."

"If he's innocent, Jennie, they'll let him go."

That's what you're afraid of, isn't it, McGrady?—that maybe they won't let him go. That they'll find evidence to convict him.

"I'll never forget the way he looked at me." Somewhere in the night her mind had rummaged through her memories and dredged up the story of Judas betraying

Jesus. She expressed her thoughts aloud.

"It's not the same," Rocky said.

"I keep telling myself that, but the picture keeps coming into my mind."

"It doesn't do any good to keep torturing yourself. You've got to let it go."

"I've tried. It's like a tune that pops in and you can't get it out."

"Then maybe you need to start singing another song."

After a long silence, Jennie sat up and swung her legs off the lounge chair. What Rocky had said made a lot of sense. She would stop beating herself up over Jerry's arrest and search for more evidence—something that would prove his innocence—or his guilt. Rocky had his eyes closed and for a moment she wondered if he were sleeping. His dark skin almost glowed in the subdued lighting. What a strange man. Tough, intense, yet warm and compassionate. He had so many sides and some of them just didn't fit.

She remembered what Lisa had said earlier. He'd called himself Robert Kennedy. Was he putting Lisa on—teasing her—or lying? With everything that had happened Jennie hadn't had an opportunity to check Mr. Beaumont's files on Rocky. She'd remedy that tomorrow.

As she stood, Rocky opened one eye. "Feeling better?"

Despite her suspicions about him, Jennie felt grateful that he'd been there. "Yeah. Thanks for listening. I think I'll be able to sleep now."

———

Allison came to Jennie and Lisa's room at eight-thirty the next morning to summon them for breakfast on the patio near the pool. A cloudless day had already warmed away last night's chill. Jennie just wished it would warm her inner chill as well.

"Where's B.J.?" Jennie asked when they joined Allison at the glass-topped, white patio table. Jennie dropped into a padded chair and poured herself a glass of orange juice.

Allison shrugged. "She was gone when I went in to wake her."

"Hi, guys." B.J. stepped out through the open patio door and approached the table. "Heard the news?" She glanced around at each of the girls. "Guess not." B.J. dropped into the vacant chair next to Jennie, picked up a slice of toast, and proceeded to drop a teaspoon of jam on it.

Jennie was beginning to feel like an overstretched rubber band. She leaned back in her chair trying to look calm. No way was Jennie going to let B.J. know she was getting to her.

"The police are here right now talking to Dad about Jerry."

Allison threw her napkin on the table and pushed her chair back. "Relax, Al," B.J. said as she poured a glass of juice. "Dad said he'd be out in a few minutes."

"Did they tell you anything?" Lisa asked.

B.J. took the newspaper from her lap and placed it on the table. "Yeah," she said. "Looks like you were wrong, McGrady. Jerry's been charged."

Allison stared at her hands.

Lisa shook her head, sending her red mane flying. "No . . . I refuse to believe it. Jerry couldn't have made those awful phone calls. He couldn't . . ." She grabbed Jennie's arm. "Remember? The night before last? The guy in the Murrays' driveway. That couldn't have been Jerry."

"I don't know." Jennie didn't want to believe in their friend's guilt either, but she felt certain the call she'd intercepted the day before in Mr. B's den had been from

Jerry. And it didn't take a mind reader to interpret his feelings for Allison. Would his frustration at not being able to date her push him to such extremes? Jennie rubbed her forehead.

"Well, I do." B.J. reached over and grabbed a second piece of bacon and took a bite. "I overheard the cop say they had a positive I.D. from the florist. He also said that Jerry admitted to sending the flowers. And get this—one of the neighbors said she noticed his truck cruising by just about every day."

Allison stood up. She had that fragile look again— like her world could crumble at any minute and she'd crash right along with it. "I don't want to hear any more. I'm going to my room." She covered her mouth to catch an escaping sob and ran into the house.

Lisa scooted back her chair and dropped her napkin on the table. "I'd better go with her." Jennie resisted the urge to follow Lisa and Allison inside; she needed to stay and talk to Donovan.

"Sheesh!" B.J. rolled her eyes in disgust. "A little over emotional, wouldn't you say?"

Jennie turned back to B.J. and took a deep breath. "You know, B.J., you're about as subtle as a rockslide. Allison has been through a lot. She could use a little sympathy. Jerry's our friend. Even if he turns out to be the stalker, which I doubt, you don't have to act so happy about it."

B.J. shrugged. "Trouble with you, McGrady, is that you're a poor loser. You just can't admit that I'm a better detective than you are. I had the guy pegged the minute he showed up here. He has the hots for Allison." B.J. huffed and added, "There's no way she'd ever go out with that cowboy. I figure he means to get her one way or the other. I remember reading this story about a guy that killed his ex-wife. Said if he couldn't have her no one else could either."

Jennie suppressed the urge to pour the rest of the orange juice on B.J.'s head. "I wouldn't be giving any victory speeches yet. Besides, I thought you suspected Rocky."

"I did, but that was before I saw Jerry."

Jennie would have liked to throttle her, but took a bite of toast instead. It all seemed like a big joke to B.J., and she was a little too quick to blame Jerry for all of this. *Maybe she's trying to keep your attention off her. Yeah, McGrady, but at least be honest with yourself. What bothers you most about B.J. is that you were thinking exactly the same thing.*

The girls finished their breakfast in silence. B.J. drained the last of her juice and set the glass down. "Why don't you think Jerry's the stalker? I mean, look at the evidence against him."

Before Jennie could answer, Beaumont, Rocky, and Greg Donovan approached the table. "Judging from what my daughter just said, I take it she told you about the Shepherd kid."

Jennie nodded.

B.J. slouched arrogantly in her chair and folded her arms across her chest. "She doesn't think he's guilty."

"Really," Donovan said, smiling down at Jennie. He lowered himself into the chair Lisa had vacated. "Why's that?"

"A hunch." After she said it she felt embarrassed. Mr. Beaumont looked at her as if he were indulging a six-year-old child with a dumb idea. Rocky just folded his arms and stood there with an expression that reminded her of a guard dog ready to pounce at any second.

Donovan, however, seemed interested in what she had to say, so she tried to ignore the others and went on. "It doesn't add up. Jerry's one of the nicest guys in school.

And he's not stupid. If he were going to stalk someone, he wouldn't order flowers from a place near where he lives and show up in person so the clerk could identify him. With the trail he left, my five-year-old brother could have tracked him down. Besides," Jennie continued, "he's not the same guy who pulled a gun on Lisa and me the night before last."

"How can you be so sure?"

"Jerry has an accent. The gunman didn't. Jerry never goes anywhere without his truck. The gunman was driving a gray sedan. Then there's the message on the mirror—he couldn't have done that."

"Mirror?" Donovan frowned.

So they hadn't called the police. Jennie opened her mouth to tell him about it when Rocky stepped forward. "An incident that happened yesterday afternoon—Beaumont doesn't think it's connected to this case."

Jennie felt her face and neck grow hot. How could he say that? She glanced over at B.J., who was not taking the news well.

"Not connected?" B.J. scrambled to her feet. Her chair scraped against the concrete pad. "What do you mean?" B.J. clenched her fists. "You think I . . ." B.J. swore and backed away.

Beaumont stepped toward her. "Bethany, it's okay, honey, I understand. Really."

"You don't understand anything. I should never have come here. I—I hate you!" B.J. spun around and ran across the lawn.

Beaumont tore out after her with Rocky at his heels.

To Jennie's surprise, Donovan remained seated. He rested his arms on the table and shifted his gaze to Jennie. "Want to tell me what that was all about?"

13

Jennie explained the relationship as best she could, then told him about the message they'd found on the mirror and how someone had later erased it. "I didn't think they'd reported it. I'd planned on calling you this morning."

Donovan nodded as if he believed her. "Do you think B.J. wrote the message on the mirror? Her father seemed pretty certain."

Jennie shrugged. "B.J. swears she didn't. I suppose she could have—you know, to get even."

"Unless she just wanted the attention."

Jennie glanced in the direction B.J. had gone, but there was no sign of her or her pursuers. "I suppose. She's sure getting plenty of that. To be honest, I've suspected B.J.'s involvement from the beginning. The only thing is, she'd have to be working with someone."

"Jerry?"

Jennie shifted her attention back to Donovan. "I don't think she knew him before last night—and like I said, Jerry's straight. She could be working with Rocky, though."

"The butler?" A smile stretched across his face.

He doesn't believe a word you're saying, McGrady. He

was probably just digging for information. Donovan reached up to rub his neck. He seemed tired, and Jennie wondered if he'd been up all night. She imagined poor Jerry sitting in a room being bombarded with questions from officers trying to make him talk. Maybe instead of giving Donovan information she should try to gather some from him. "B.J. told us Jerry confessed," Jennie said. "Is that true?"

"Partly, yes. He admitted to sending Allison flowers on three different occasions and to calling her last night. Denies knowing anything about the threats."

Jennie drummed her fingers on the tabletop. A thought that had been scrambling around in her head finally settled to within reach. "Do you think it's possible that we're dealing with two people here?" Once the words spilled out, they made perfect sense. "Suppose Jerry's plan to send Allison flowers just happened to coincide with someone else's plan to stalk her? Isn't that possible?"

"Possible—yes, likely—no."

To Jennie it seemed the only logical answer. "Why not?"

Greg shoved a hand through his already tousled hair. "My guess is the guy deliberately set us up—wants us to think there are two guys. It's an old trick. Probably figures we won't be able to pin the rest on him and he'll get off." Greg shook his head. "He's even reading the Bible— as if that'll make us think he's basically a good guy. D.A. thinks we've got another religious fanatic. A lot of those nuts running around these days. Carry a Bible in one hand and a .38 in the other."

Jennie squirmed uncomfortably in her chair. Could Donovan be right? Jerry openly declared his faith. His free use of Scripture and what she termed "God talk" had embarrassed her more than once.

Still, Jerry seemed so sincere. He was always helping people. Jennie closed her eyes, remembering the time not long ago when he'd given her and Lisa a ride home from a youth meeting. On the seat lay a brown, well-used, leather-bound Bible, but on a rack attached to the back window hung a hunting rifle. Still, deep inside, Jennie couldn't see Jerry Shepherd as a stalker. *But he's in jail right now, McGrady, and you helped put him there.*

"You seem convinced Jerry is guilty," Jennie said. "Why did you ask me what I thought?"

Donovan shrugged. "Just trying to cover all the angles."

The sliding glass door of the patio shooshed open. Rocky stepped out and walked toward them. Ignoring Jennie and looking directly at Donovan, he said, "Mr. Beaumont asked me to apologize for the . . . uh, incident involving his daughter. He'll come down to the station later and press charges."

"I'll be leaving then," Donovan said. "Thanks for your help. Keep me posted." He stopped at the door. "Oh, and, Jennie, your friend is being arraigned this afternoon at the county courthouse. Around one. He's second on the docket."

After Donovan left, Rocky glanced at Jennie and smiled. "Looks like you're feeling better this morning."

"I am. I've taken your advice. I'm singing a different tune. This one says Jerry isn't the stalker. Like I told Donovan, I think we're dealing with two different people, and I'm going to find out who the other one is."

Rocky frowned and stroked his chin. "I wouldn't sing that song too loudly, Jennie, or you just might end up in an alley with your throat slit."

If he'd meant to scare her he had, but she was determined not to show it. "Thanks for the advice, but I can take care of myself. I . . . think I'll go see how Allison and Lisa are doing," Jennie stammered as she took a step back, then turned and walked slowly toward the house.

"Don't do anything stupid," he called to her retreating figure. Jennie didn't look back. She could feel his eyes boring into her. *Nice going, McGrady. Why didn't you just tell him you suspected him at the same time so he could have killed you right then and there?* On the other hand, she decided, maybe telling him her plans hadn't been such a bad idea. She'd certainly gotten a reaction. The only problem now was how to read it. Had the strong response she'd gotten been meant as a warning from someone who cared? Or had it been a threat?

Once inside she broke into a run. She found Lisa and Allison near the window in her bedroom. Allison had been crying. Lisa looked worried. "We saw you talking to Officer Donovan. What did you find out?"

"Did they really charge Jerry with stalking?" Allison asked.

"Yeah." Jennie twirled a strand of hair around her forefinger. "He's being arraigned this afternoon. I'm going down to see him. Give him his hat. See if there's anything I can do."

"I'd like to go along," Allison offered.

"Me too." Lisa stood. "When?"

"About one. Um . . . there's something you need to know, Allison." Jennie paused then added, "Jerry's admitted to sending you flowers and to calling last night."

"No . . ." Allison closed her eyes. "It can't be true."

"Are you saying he's the stalker?" Lisa asked, falling back into her chair.

"No, I'm saying he sent flowers and wrote the love notes. I think we're dealing with two different people here. I can't see Jerry sending dead flowers or making threats, and I'm sure he wasn't the one who pulled a gun on Lisa and me the other night. And if Jerry didn't do it, there has to be another guy."

"Of course!" Allison said, looking relieved. Then casting Jennie a questioning look, asked, "He sent me flowers?"

Jennie sat on the arm of Lisa's chair. "Did you know he liked you?"

Allison rose from her bed and walked to the window. "I kind of suspected it, but . . ."

Jennie braced herself, thinking Allison might laugh at the idea.

Allison turned back to them. "I just never dreamed a guy as sweet as Jerry would ever care about someone like me."

"You mean you like him?" The words had tumbled out before she could stop them. *And you accused B.J. of not being subtle.*

"Why is that so hard to believe? I've had a crush on Jerry since junior high. I just never imagined . . . He's so outgoing and popular . . . to be honest I never thought I had a chance."

Lisa gave Jennie her famous I-told-you-so look.

Jennie relented. "Okay, I'll admit. I was wrong."

"Wrong about what? What are you talking about?" Allison asked.

Jennie took a deep breath and started picking at the frayed edge of her cutoffs. "I was wrong about you, and I owe you an apology. When Lisa first asked me to help you, I didn't want to get involved. I thought you were a snob."

Jennie sneaked a look at her cousin, who smiled and gave her a thumbs-up sign. "Lisa tried to tell me, but I didn't listen. Anyway, I'm sorry. If anybody is a snob, it's me. I jumped to the wrong conclusions."

"Don't feel too bad, Jennie. A lot of people get the wrong idea about me—my dad says, 'When you have money folks either hang around, hoping it will rub off, or find something wrong with you.' Anyway, don't worry about it. I don't think either you or Lisa are like that." Allison heaved a deep sigh. "We've got a party to get ready for and . . ." Her eyes clouded. "The party. How can I even think about a party when Jerry's in jail? Maybe I should call it off."

"No," Jennie said. "Don't do that. If I'm right about the real stalker still being out there, he . . . or she may show up at the party. I'd like to talk to a few people— get their reactions. Oh, and speaking of reactions, you should have seen the rise I got out of Rocky." Jennie filled them in on what Rocky had said. "Allison, tonight during the party I'd like to have a look in your dad's office. Is that possible?"

Allison's brow furrowed. "I don't know. Maybe during dinner. Daddy will be grilling hamburgers and hot dogs for everyone. He'll be busy for quite a while doing that."

"Good. I'll eat early then go in. I'll need you to cover for me."

While Lisa stayed behind to help Allison get ready for the party, Jennie went to look for B.J. She found her in the kitchen with Mrs. Beaumont. "Oh, hi, Jennie," Mrs. B. said cheerfully. "Come on in and join us. We're just making a vegetable tray for the party."

"Be careful, McGrady, or she'll put you to work making radish roses."

Mrs. Beaumont smiled. "Don't let her fool you, Jennie. She's loving every minute of this."

"Right," B.J. countered. "It's almost as much fun as cutting my toenails."

Jennie eyed the "roses" lined up on the counter. "They look great. I wish I could stay and help, but I need to go home to change and run a couple of errands. I just wanted to see if you were okay, B.J., and tell you that I'm meeting Allison and Lisa at the courthouse this afternoon for Jerry's arraignment. Want to come?"

B.J. shrugged, set a finished radish aside, picked up another, and sliced into it. "Ask the warden."

Mrs. B. came up to B.J. and draped her arm around the girl's shoulder. "This isn't a prison, sweetheart. It's a home."

B.J. shrugged away. "Yeah, and the door's open. I can leave anytime I want. Like *dear Daddy* says, I have two choices—I either stay here and follow his stupid rules, or I go to a foster home. Well there's one more option—the street—and right now that's starting to look pretty good."

B.J. tossed down the knife and radish and walked out. The radish rolled across the counter. Jennie caught it as it fell off. "Well, are you coming or not?" she yelled after B.J.

"No!" B.J. yelled back. A few seconds later a door slammed. Jennie glanced at Mrs. Beaumont.

"I'm sorry, Jennie. Bethany is going through a lot right now."

So who isn't? Jennie felt like saying. Instead she made a suggestion that surprised even her. "I don't know if it would help, but maybe you should all see a counselor."

Jennie could almost feel the frost settling on the room. "Thank you, Jennie, but I don't think that will be necessary."

Jennie rummaged through her brain for a suitable exit line. Fortunately, Allison and Lisa came to the rescue, and Jennie was able to make her getaway.

Instead of going straight home, Jennie stopped at Crystal Springs, a large parklike garden near her home. She parked in the small lot, slipped a dollar into the donation box, and walked down the flower-lined path to a bridge that spanned a small lake and led to an island. Jennie found her favorite bench by the water and sank onto it.

She watched a couple of trumpeter swans lazily glide through the water. "You two sure have it easy," she said softly, so as not to disturb them. "Want to trade places?" She smiled as one of the swans dipped its head. "I don't blame you. This case has more loose ends than a mop doll." She thought about all the possibilities and shuddered.

"Who is it, God?" she whispered. "Who's stalking Allison?" B.J. definitely had an attitude problem. Rocky was hiding something, and Jennie had a hunch it was more than his name.

A twig snapped. Rocky's words jammed into her brain. *You might find yourself in an alley with your throat slit. Or,* Jennie added, *in a park.*

14

Jennie could hardly hear over the pounding of her heart as she rose and turned toward the direction of the sound. A squirrel scurried up the path, then disappeared into the bushes. *You're getting paranoid, McGrady. There's no one here.* Or maybe they just hadn't found her. The bench sat off the main path, hidden behind a thick grove of rhododendrons. One thing for sure, she wasn't about to wait around long enough to find out. Jennie hurried back the way she'd come, not stopping until she reached the parking lot. There, parked next to her white Mustang was a gray sedan.

She patted her pockets for the keys. Empty. Panic tightened its long tentacles around her and left her gasping for breath. She'd locked the keys in the car. Jennie tried the doors. Locked. Why couldn't she just this once have forgotten to lock one of them?

Oh, God, what am I going to do? The answer came in a split second. *Run!*

Jennie reached the house in less than three minutes. No one was home. She tore around the back of the house and retrieved their spare key from under a large redwood planter and let herself in. A note on the counter told her Mom had gone shopping and Aunt Kate had taken Kurt and Nick to the zoo. She found the spare set of keys on their hook by the back door and started to return to her car, then stopped. *Not smart, McGrady. What if he's still there?* Jennie called the police and asked for Donovan. When they patched her through, she told him about the gray car. "I'll bet anything the stalker is there right now."

"Stay where you are. We're on our way," Donovan ordered.

After she hung up, Jennie threw her keys in the air and caught them. *Great job, McGrady,* she congratulated herself. *In a few minutes they'll nab the real stalker and you'll have solved another mystery. Well, sort of. At any rate, it will be over.* "I'll bet it's Rocky," she mused. *Or B.J. . . . Or . . .*

While she waited, Jennie raided the refrigerator. She glanced at the digital clock on the microwave. It was 11:45. She retrieved a can of pop, a nectarine, a leftover chicken breast, then took her lunch out to the dining room where she could watch the street. She'd just taken a bite of chicken when Donovan and Mendoza drove up.

Jennie hurried out to the curb. "Did you find him?" Her words died as she noticed the empty backseat. "Did he get away?"

Officer Mendoza raised a dark eyebrow then turned to his partner. "Do you want to tell her or should I?"

"Go ahead," Donovan said as he drummed his fingers on the steering wheel.

Mendoza shifted his attention back to Jennie. "The car was still there. Turned out to be an elderly couple taking a stroll."

"Oh," Jennie squeaked. "I thought . . ." A warm flush crept through her. She stared down at the tip of her shoe.

"No," Donovan said gruffly. "That's the trouble, Jennie. You didn't think. You should never have gone into that place alone. What if it had been a stalker?"

"I'm sorry." Jennie looked back into their car, being careful to avoid eye contact.

Mendoza gave her a forgiving grin. "We don't mind the false alarm so much, Jennie. That was an honest mistake. But next time you go out, take someone with you and leave your imagination behind."

When they'd gone, Jennie entered the house feeling totally defeated. Donovan's reproof echoed in her head. *You didn't think.* It was true, she hadn't. Mom and Gram would probably have said the same thing—only they wouldn't have been as quick to forgive. But after the lectures they'd have sat down with her and had a cup of tea and talked about it until Jennie felt human again. Since neither of them was there, Jennie decided to make some peppermint tea anyway. Over tea and the rest of her lunch she tried to imagine how Gram would have reacted to her blunder.

"There, there," she'd croon. "Don't take it so hard, my girl. We all make mistakes. Next time you'll know better."

Would she? It had been a dumb move. She knew better than to go into the park alone, but she'd been preoccupied.

Jennie held the steaming mug in both hands, relishing the warmth. She took a sip of the warm brew and concentrated on the minty aroma and the way the steam caressed her face. Closing her eyes, Jennie imagined Gram sitting across the table. Salt and pepper hair framing a slightly wrinkled face and dark blue eyes.

Jennie paused to wipe away an errant tear. "Oh,

Gram, I miss you. Hurry home."

After cleaning up her lunch leavings, Jennie jogged back to the park to get her car. As she reached the Mustang, an older couple emerged from the garden entrance. Jennie watched them walk to the gray car. Must have been the couple Donovan and Mendoza had seen. Only it couldn't be. The gray car she'd seen had been parked right next to hers. Dread trickled through her veins like ice water.

"Excuse me," Jennie called to the elderly man as he opened the passenger door for his wife. "How long have you been here?"

The man glanced at his watch. "Oh," he rasped, "'bout thirty minutes . . . wouldn't you say, Mama?"

The woman nodded. "Takes us about that long to walk through. Do it every day. When you get to be our age, you have to stay in shape."

Jennie smiled. Gram would like these people. "Did you talk to the police earlier?"

"Nope," the old man answered. "Saw 'em though. Looked like they were after someone."

"Ummm . . . one more thing. When you came in, was there a gray car like yours parked over there, next to mine?"

The man drew an age-spotted hand across his mouth. "Don't recall that, but I did see a gray car. Just as we were turning in here. In such a hurry he 'bout run us over. Headed back that way." He pointed north.

Jennie let out the breath she'd been holding. Her house was four blocks south. She managed a thank you, climbed into her car, and drove back home. By the time she'd gotten to the house, Jennie had convinced herself that the man had not been after her. The gray car parked next to hers meant nothing. Metallic gray, newer model, Oregon plates. Thousands of people owned gray cars. It had been a coincidence. After all, if he'd been after her, wouldn't he have headed toward her house rather than away from it? *But what about the license plate, McGrady? How many gray cars have plates with two zeros at the end?*

A memory of the stalker's phone call eased out of its cell and hung in her mind like a ghostly apparition. *Tell Allison she can't escape. Wherever she goes, whatever she does. I'll be there. And if you and that snoopy cousin of yours try to stop me, I'll get you too.*

At that moment Mom pulled into the driveway and Jennie shooed the unwanted memory back into hiding.

"Oh, Jennie, I'm glad you're home." Mom staggered through the back door with a bag of groceries and a box of laundry detergent the size of a football field. "You can help me bring in the groceries."

"Oh goodie, my favorite thing to do." Jennie grabbed the box and deposited it in the laundry room off the kitchen, then followed her mother out to the car and reached into the trunk for a couple of bags. "Whoa, what'd you do, invite the whole neighborhood to dinner?"

Mom laughed. "Not quite. Some of this stuff is for the camping trip. And Michael will be eating meals with us for the next few days while his landlord remodels his kitchen."

The news excited Jennie about as much as eating raw liver, but she wasn't about to argue. Besides, the solution was simple enough. She'd just spend the next few days with Lisa. Even though the idea rankled, Jennie couldn't resist a jibe. "Mom, Michael's a guy—you know, a homo-sapien—not an elephant."

"I know, I just wanted to be sure I had enough."

They carried the groceries in and began stashing them. "I'll help you put these away, Mom, but then I've got to get going." She explained about Jerry's arrest and arraignment.

Jennie pulled a couple cans of tomato sauce from the sack and stacked them in the cupboard. "I don't think he's the stalker."

"That's what Michael says."

"Michael?" Jennie paused. "What does Michael have to do with it?"

"Jerry called him last night after he'd been arrested. Michael's been working with him and his mother ever since—getting a lawyer, arranging bail. He told me about it when he came by for breakfast this morning."

"He's a regular Clark Kent, isn't he? Bet he's got a great big *S* tattooed on his chest."

"Jennie." Mom frowned and tossed a bag of marshmallows on the counter. "That was uncalled for. Michael cares about people. Besides, like he told me, he's the youth director now and the kids need him." Her voice trailed off.

"I know. But he's always around. A month ago I didn't even know Michael Rhodes, now I feel like I can't even brush my teeth without having him tell me when to spit."

Mom tipped her head. "Isn't that a slight exaggeration?"

"Mom, the man actually signed me up for the youth retreat. Where does he get off?"

"You can't blame Michael for that. I told him you were coming with us. Michael just passed the information along to Jerry." Mom heaved a sigh that seemed to come from her toes. "Don't fight me on this, Jennie. It isn't easy for me either. There are times when I'm so sure I've made the right decision to marry him. Other times . . . I just don't know."

"You mean you're having second thoughts? You might not get married?" All of a sudden Jennie wanted to hear more. Outside she tried to look calm and concerned. Inside she was doing cartwheels and jumping up and down yelling, *Yes! Yes! Yes!*

Mom tore open a bag of chips and ate one. "I don't know. I love Michael. I'm just not sure we're right for each other."

"Why?"

Mom took the chips to the table, sat down, and slipped her shoes off. Jennie eased into the seat next to her. "It's hard to explain. Michael is the sweetest, dearest man I've ever known. He's thoughtful and considerate." She paused to nibble on another chip. "I suppose I'm being selfish. I don't mean to be, but lately he's been spending so much time at the church and with the kids. Oh, I know a new job takes extra time, but . . . I guess I'm afraid he's going to become so consumed by his work he won't have time for family."

Jennie stiffened. Mom wasn't just talking about Michael anymore. She was criticizing Dad. Jennie started to object when her mother spoke again.

"I'm sure it will work out. At least he assures me it will. At any rate, since we asked you to set the date, I thought you should know. I, ah . . ." Mom got up and headed back to the groceries still littering the counter, but not before Jennie noticed the tears forming in her eyes. "I told Michael I wanted to wait for at least a year. I think I'll need at least that long, maybe longer. I don't want to make the same . . . Well, never mind. I know you're anxious to get to court so you'd better get ready."

. . . *Didn't want to make the same mistake again.* That's what her mom had started to say. Jennie vacillated between being upset with her for putting Dad down and rejoicing over the delay in wedding plans. She finally decided on being happy. As soon as she reached her room she picked up her dad's picture. "Looks like we got a reprieve, Pop. Now all I have to do is find you." A voice from somewhere deep inside dampened her joy with a harsh reminder. *You may not find him, McGrady. And even if you do, there's no guarantee your mom will take him back. Or that he'll come home.*

Jennie pushed the negative thoughts aside and glanced at her watch. One o'clock. Fifteen minutes later Jennie did one last mirror check—white tailored shirt, clean jeans, loafers, hair, eyes—"Yep, they're all there." She grabbed her purse, keys, and Jerry's hat and headed downtown to the courthouse.

The arraignment process had already begun. Jennie slipped in through the double doors at the back of the courtroom. Lisa, Allison, and Mr. Beaumont were sitting in the second row behind Jerry. Two rows behind them were Paige and Eddie. Rocky sat on an aisle row to her left, three rows from the back. A lot of people for an arraignment, and Jennie had a hunch they weren't all there to lend support.

Not wanting to disrupt the proceedings by walking up front, Jennie took the aisle seat in the back row. It wasn't until the man next to her touched her arm that she realized she was sitting next to Michael. He smiled and leaned his head toward hers. "Jerry will be glad to see you. He needs all the support he can get."

Jennie closed her eyes and nodded. Weird. That was

the best word Jennie could come up with to describe her feelings at that moment. She wasn't angry at Michael for being there. She didn't feel annoyed that once again he'd interfered in her life. Actually, she was glad. Jerry did need all the help he could get. In fact, she didn't feel much of anything—except maybe thankfulness that Michael had been there for Jerry. Amazing what a little talk with one's mother could do.

"What's going on?" Jennie whispered as she watched two men in suits talking in hushed tones to the judge.

"I'm not sure. I think his lawyer is trying to get the case dismissed. That's going to be tough though. When the police searched Jerry's truck they found a tube of red lipstick and Mr. Beaumont's missing gun in the glove box."

15

"Someone framed him," Jennie told Officer Donovan when she caught up with him on the courthouse steps. "And I can prove it." She dug through her oversized leather bag and produced a plastic bag containing the lipstick she'd found in Allison's bathroom. "I don't know where the tube came from that you found in Jerry's truck, but this is the one that was used to write the message on Allison's mirror. I . . . um . . . I meant to give it to you yesterday and forgot."

The corner of Donovan's mouth twitched as though he were trying to keep a straight face. "Quite the detective, aren't you? Even bagged it. Unfortunately, it doesn't prove a thing."

"But I found it . . ."

"Jennie . . ." Donovan ran a hand through his hair and stroked his head as though he were trying to stimulate his mind for the right words. "I believe you. It's just not the kind of evidence that would hold up in court. Who's to say you didn't just buy it to help your friend out? Now, if you'd turned it in right away it might have made a difference."

Jennie winced. "I meant to, but . . . I guess it doesn't matter. I blew it." Jennie handed him the bag. "Couldn't

116

you at least check it for fingerprints?"

Donovan took the bag and examined it. "Probably wouldn't do much good. It's hard to get good prints off something like this." He lowered his arm. "Besides, it's not the lipstick that will convict your friend. It's the gun."

"But if someone planted the lipstick, doesn't it make sense that the gun was planted as well?"

"I'm sorry, Jennie—for you and your friend. It's always hard to accept the fact that someone you know has committed a crime. But as far as the department is concerned the case is closed."

Jennie started to tell him about her discussion with the elderly couple and the other gray car, but didn't. He wouldn't have believed her anyway. *The investigation may be over for you, but as far as I'm concerned it has only just begun.* Jennie hadn't made the statement aloud, but Donovan seemed to have heard it anyway. "Don't be doing anything foolish, Jennie."

Jennie glared at him and walked away, pausing at the last step. She glanced up at the courthouse doors, wondering whether or not to go back inside. The judge had released Jerry into Michael's custody and had set bail at $10,000. As soon as the papers were signed and the bail bond paid, Jerry would be free to go home. She wished they'd hurry.

The sound of muffled voices caught her attention. Donovan and Rocky were standing near the corner of the building. Jennie paused for a moment to watch them. She was too far away to hear what they were saying, but their gestures and the scowl on Rocky's face told her they were arguing. About what? At that moment Rocky's gaze caught hers. The anger in his eyes flickered and died like the blaze on a birthday candle. Jennie glanced away.

When she looked back Donovan was walking toward the parking lot, and Rocky had joined the group coming out of the courthouse. Allison appeared first, with Jerry on one arm and her father on the other. Lisa and Michael came out right behind them, then Paige and Eddie.

"Daddy, please," Allison pleaded. "Let me stay and talk to him for a few minutes."

"I'd rather you came home with me."

"I'll be fine." She glanced around. Her gaze settled on Jennie. "Jennie and Lisa will bring me home. I'll be safe with them."

Mr. B. looked at Jennie. The weariness and indecision in his eyes startled her. "It's okay, Mr. Beaumont," Jennie said, hoping she was doing the right thing. "Lisa and I will see that she gets home okay."

Mr. B. nodded. "All right, but don't be too long." He moved along the step to where Rocky stood and started talking to him in hushed tones. He was probably telling Rocky to make certain they got back okay, Jennie decided. She made a mental note to talk with Mr. B. later, then turned her attention back to the others.

Jerry had somehow extricated himself from Allison's grip and was shaking Michael's hand. "Thanks. I don't know what I would have done without your help."

Michael pulled Jerry into an embrace and patted his back, then released him. "Just glad we were able to get you out."

"I'll pay ya'll back. . . . I mean it. You too, Eddie. If you guys hadn't come up with the bail money . . . I don't know what I'd have done. Mom needs me at the farm and . . ."

"Hey, man," Eddie said as he squeezed Jerry's shoulder, "what are friends for? You've come through for me plenty of times on the court."

Jennie frowned. While Eddie and Jerry had played basketball together, she'd never noticed them being especially close. Had something happened recently to change that? Looked like she'd be asking a lot of questions at the party tonight.

"Eddie . . ." Paige tentatively touched his sleeve. "We have an appointment, remember?"

Jennie caught a brief look of annoyance in his features, but by the time he'd turned to face Paige, they'd softened. He glanced at his watch. "We'll make it." He reached out to shake Michael's hand. "Been thinking about what you said yesterday, and . . . well, me and Paige decided we'd like to go to that retreat your church is having."

Michael pumped Eddie's hand. "That's great. I know you'll have a good time."

When Paige and Eddie had gone, Jerry turned to Jennie. He smiled broadly. "See you brought my hat."

Jennie glanced down at her hand. "Yeah. Thought you might need it." She plopped it on his head and reached out to hug him. Behind the cheerful attitude and ready smile, Jennie could read the worry in his eyes. She squeezed his hand to let him know she understood.

Allison took Jerry's arm again and drew him away as if laying claim to him. Jennie smiled at that. Allison didn't need to worry about her.

"Jerry," Allison said, "I want you to come to the party tonight."

"I don't know if I can. I got a lot of work to do at home. Besides, parties aren't exactly my thing."

"Please come. I'd really like you to be there."

"But what about your dad? He's been really nice . . . even helped with the bail money. Michael talked to him, but I don't think he trusts me."

"Well, I do." She stood on her toes and kissed his cheek. "Call me later."

"I hate to break this up, kids," Michael said as he rested a hand on Jerry's shoulder. "We'd better clear out of here before they arrest all of us for loitering."

Since the police were still holding Jerry's truck, Jennie offered him a ride home. "I'll take him," Michael insisted. "I need to talk with Mrs. Shepherd about some things."

A few minutes later, Jennie buckled her seat belt and put the Mustang in reverse. "I take it you and Jerry got things straightened out," Jennie said to Allison's reflection in the rearview mirror.

Allison nodded. "Lisa and I came in to see him after you left this morning. He explained what had happened." She paused to tuck some glistening strands of hair behind her ear. "I feel so awful. I can't imagine why he'd get the idea I wouldn't like him. Do you guys really think I act like a snob?"

"Of course not," Lisa soothed. "It's just because you're shy. Jennie has the same problem."

"What do you mean?" Jennie's defenses sprang to attention. "I don't have a problem."

"Sure you do," Lisa said, lifting her heavy curls off her neck. "Well, it's not a problem exactly. It's just your personality." Lisa laughed and turned back to Allison. "Gram says I'm a social butterfly. She calls Jennie an eagle because she's more cautious."

Jennie pulled out of the parking space and eased into the traffic. Now that she knew where Lisa was going with it, she played along. "Which simply means I usually get to know people before I make a fool of myself, whereas my dear cousin here . . ."

Lisa playfully socked Jennie's arm. "Which means," she corrected, "you avoid talking to people you don't know very well, they think you're either a snob or that you don't like them."

Jennie eyed Allison in the mirror again. She'd apparently tuned out their banter. "Allison?" Jennie asked. "Are you all right?"

"What?" Allison made brief eye contact then looked away. "Oh . . . I'm okay. Just worried about Jerry. I know he hasn't done anything wrong. But how in the world are we going to prove it?"

Allison's question burrowed itself in Jennie's mind like a stubborn tick. *You've solved mysteries before,* she kept reminding herself, *you can solve this one as well.*

Since the party was scheduled to start at four-thirty, the girls had barely enough time to get ready. The party had basically two stages. The first part included talking, swimming, and a barbecue. Later, around seven-thirty or eight, they'd go up to the guest bedrooms, one set up for the boys, the other for the girls, and change into dress clothes for a formal candlelight dessert. The Beaumonts had hired a local band to provide the entertainment.

Jerry arrived at four. Since Allison was busy helping set up the pool area, Jennie let him in. "I wasn't going to come," he admitted, "but Michael talked me into it. Said it might be good for me—take my mind off my troubles. He took me home and helped me do some chores, then brought me back." Jerry held up a garment bag and guitar case. "Allison told me to bring these. Where do I stash 'em?"

Jennie led the way to the boys' guest room and opened the closet door. "You're lucky, Jen," he said over his shoulder as he hung up his clothes.

"Me?"

"Yeah. Your mom marrying Michael and all. He'll make a great stepdad."

Jennie couldn't think of anything to say. Her usual caustic thoughts didn't come, and that bothered her. Was her attitude toward Michael changing? Was she starting to accept him? *No,* she reasoned. *You just don't have to worry about him anymore. The more Michael gets involved in his work, the less likely Mom will be to marry him.* Jennie smiled. "Yep. He's a regular Clark Kent."

When she took Jerry back downstairs, Allison practically tackled him. After introducing him to her mom, she put him to work carrying trays of food out to the tables they'd placed around the patio. From four-thirty to five a steady stream of kids poured in. Jennie stopped counting at thirty. According to Allison, during the course of the evening they'd have about a hundred—too many people for Jennie to deal with at one time. She fought back the urge to go home by reminding herself she had people to talk to and a certain file to read.

After playing volleyball and cooling off in the pool, Jennie went in to change out of her suit. When she came back downstairs she caught Mr. Beaumont coming out of his office. *Perfect timing, McGrady. Talk to him.* Right— but what would she say? *Hey, Mr. B., I'm investigating your daughter's case. Wonder if we could have a chat.* No, that wouldn't work. She couldn't let him know what she was doing. He'd probably kick her out. Jennie wished she could talk as well to others as she did to herself. She held up a hand to stop him. "Mr. Beaumont." Well at least she'd gotten that much out. "I was hoping to get a chance to talk with you."

"Sure, Jennie. Come on into my office."

He showed Jennie into an office that had the same rich wood as his den downstairs. He directed her to a wing-backed chair the color of dried blood. *Dried blood?* Where in the world had that macabre description come from? Probably one of the mysteries she was always reading. Or maybe the spooky darkness of this room. *Stop it, Mc-Grady.* "Nice room," she said, glancing around to familiarize herself with it.

Mr. B. went behind his desk and stopped at the window. In an instant the vertical shades opened, slicing away the darkness. "That's better," he said, moving back toward her and sitting in the maroon chair beside her. "Now, what can I do for you?"

16

Jennie contemplated several openings, then settled on, "I heard you helped post bail for Jerry today. I wanted to thank you. He's a good friend."

Mr. B. nodded.

"You must be sure he isn't the real stalker."

"I'm not sure of anything, Jennie." He sighed. "Allison and Michael are convinced. The boy has no criminal record. He's been an exemplary student; so I guess until or unless the police prove otherwise . . ." His sentence faded.

"I believe in Jerry too—at least I want to," Jennie said, "but I can't help wondering about the evidence they found in his truck. That was your gun, wasn't it?"

"Yes, from my collection."

"Any idea who might have taken it?"

Mr. B. tipped his head and cocked an eyebrow. "Why all the questions?"

Jennie dug her fingers into the chair arms. Should she tell him the truth and risk getting thrown out, or should she feign simple curiosity and risk the same? Earlier she'd suspected Mr. Beaumont; now her intuition told her he was just as much a victim as Allison. Drawing in a deep breath, Jennie decided to tell him the truth. "This might sound kind of strange, Mr. B., but Allison asked me to help find the stalker."

"Allison . . . you?" he sputtered.

"Wait a second, Mr. B., let me explain."

"This better be good."

"I'm not a private detective or anything, but I plan to study law in college . . . let me put it this way. My grandfather, Ian McGrady, was with the FBI. So was—is my father. My grandmother, Helen McGrady, used to be a police officer. Ever since I was a kid, she and I would take cases from the paper and try to solve them before the police did. Gram taught me a lot. Anyway, I've solved a couple of real cases . . ."

"And you think you can solve this one?" Mr. B. looked even more weary. "I'm sorry, Jennie. You're only a child. I can't let you jeopardize your life, or the investigation, by letting you get involved in something like this. We're dealing with a stalker here. A man threatening murder. I know you want to help, but if you insist on playing these detective games, I'll have to ask you to leave." He dragged his hand down his face. "Allison asked you to help?"

Jennie nodded. "She said you weren't taking this seriously. She was afraid . . ."

"Not taking . . ." He shook his head in disbelief. "I told her there was nothing to worry about because I didn't want her to be upset." Returning his gaze to Jennie, he said, "I'm sorry she dragged you into this. I'll have a talk with her. The police are doing an adequate job. Now I suggest you go back to the party and have fun."

"All right, but can I make a suggestion?"

"What's that?"

"Have the police check out Rocky. I suspect he's

working under an assumed name. He told Lisa his name was Robert Kennedy."

"I'm afraid your detective skills aren't as finely tuned as you seem to think, young lady. You're wrong about Rocky. I check out all my employees. His references are impeccable." Mr. B. glanced at his watch. "Was that all you wanted?"

His words had cut deep, but Jennie tried not to let it show. "I did want to ask how B.J. was doing. After this morning . . . I mean . . . she seemed pretty upset."

Pain flickered in his eyes, and Jennie saw the same weariness she'd witnessed on the courthouse steps. He rubbed at his brow.

"Never mind," Jennie began, "it's none of my business. I shouldn't have asked—"

"No, it's okay. There's no point in hiding it. You'll find out soon enough anyway. Bethany's gone. She's at Children's Services waiting for placement in a foster home."

"Oh, no." Jennie leaned forward and rested her hand on his arm. "I'm so sorry." It had been an automatic response, but the moment Jennie realized what she'd done she slowly pulled her hand away.

He didn't seem to notice. "My wife said you'd suggested we see a counselor. Looks like we'll be doing just that. Just hope it's not too late."

"B.J. will come around. She just needs time to adjust. It hasn't been that long since her mom died. My dad's been gone for five years and . . ." *It's different, McGrady. Dad's not dead.* "Just trust me, Mr. Beaumont. It takes a long time."

As Jennie left his office an outrageous idea began to form in her mind. *Oh, no, McGrady. You don't really want to do this. The last thing you need right now is another project.*

Underneath all the objections Jennie heard another stronger voice. *B.J. needs a friend. Maybe you can help.*

She'd had experience with this particular voice before. Gram said it was an inner voice—God's Spirit in us, prompting us to do good. Jennie wasn't sure about that. All she knew was that the voice didn't give up easily.

She picked up the phone and called Michael, then told him about B.J., briefly filling him in. "I was just wondering if you'd go see her, talk to her. And . . . um . . . Michael, tell her if she wants she can stay with us for a while. That is, if it's okay with Mom."

"There, I've done it," she muttered to the persistent voice as she hung up the phone. "I hope you're happy."

Despite her reservations, Jennie could feel a warm glow start from somewhere deep inside and work its way out. Jennie made her way back to the party. It took her several minutes to spot Lisa, Brad, Allison, and Jerry at the far end of the pool. She began weaving around the bodies, and about five conversations and updates on several good friends later, Jennie finally reached her goal. "Hi, Jennie." Allison grinned and motioned for her to sit in the empty chair between her and Lisa. "Daddy's about to put the hamburgers on."

"Great, I'm starved." Brad patted his stomach.

"You're always starved," Lisa teased as she poked him in the stomach. He jumped to his feet, whisked Lisa out of her chair, and dumped her in the pool. A couple of seconds later Lisa surfaced, sputtering, "Brad, you come back here. I'll get you for that."

Jennie laughed. "She will, too. I'd watch my back for a while if I were you." The words brought some not so distant memories tumbling into her mind. She remembered the fun she'd had with Scott in the pool at Dolphin

Island. Longing filled her—for the easy companionship they'd enjoyed. *It would be fun to have Scott here.* It would be even more fun to have Ryan. *Face it, McGrady. You'd just like to have a date.*

"You okay?" Lisa laid a dripping hand on Jennie's shoulder.

Jennie brushed the memories away. "I'm fine. At least I was until you got me all wet."

You don't have time for men. You've got work to do. Jennie had planned on eating before going into Beaumont's office, but the mounting anxiety over what she was about to do had obliterated her appetite. Mr. B. had called Rocky a fine, upstanding citizen. If that were true, Jennie was a washout as a detective. Her instincts told her Rocky—alias Robert Kennedy—or whatever his name was, was hiding something. And she intended to find out what.

Jennie glanced around. "Where's Rocky?" Even though Mr. B. was occupied, Jennie did not want to chance running into the object of her investigation.

"I saw him over by the grill talking to Daddy a few minutes ago." *Now?* Allison mouthed.

Jennie nodded. "I hope you guys don't mind, but I need to talk to Lisa and Allison alone for a sec."

"Go ahead." Brad turned to Jerry. "You turning out for football this year?"

"Hope to . . ." Their voices faded as Jennie walked away. It amazed her how quickly guys could shift from girls to sports.

In hushed tones, Jennie told them about the conversation she'd had with Allison's dad. She didn't mention what she'd learned about B.J. There'd be time enough for that later. Besides, Jennie had a hunch their parents hadn't told Allison, and she didn't want to be the one to break the news.

"I'm going to see if I can find Rocky's file, then I'm out. Shouldn't need more than about fifteen, twenty minutes. I shouldn't be doing this, but I have to know."

Lisa and Allison promised to keep Rocky and Beaumont out of the house to give Jennie the time she needed to find and examine Rocky's personnel file.

Just as she reached Mr. Beaumont's office, the doorbell rang. Jennie debated whether or not to answer, then realized she'd better or someone would come in to answer it. She swung open the door. "Paige. Eddie."

"Sorry we're late." Eddie's voice was tight and clipped.

Paige stepped in behind Eddie, her lips pinched so tight they looked like they'd been glued shut.

"Don't worry about it," Jennie assured them. "They're just starting the hamburgers." Jennie was no expert on human nature, but it didn't take a psychiatrist to see they'd been arguing. Under Paige's carefully applied makeup, Jennie could make out the pasty complexion and the telltale puffiness of a first-class cry.

She pretended not to notice as she told them where to put their things. Jennie watched them mount the steps and disappear down the hall, and couldn't help wondering if the "appointment" Paige had mentioned earlier that afternoon had anything to do with their distress. The word *pregnant* passed through Jennie's brain, but she dismissed the idea. Paige had too much going for her to fall into that trap.

Jennie deliberated over whether or not to wait for them to come down before going into Beaumont's office. They made the decision for her. After only a few seconds they descended the stairs hand in hand. Eddie rubbed his stomach. "I smell food. Lead me to it." Paige laughed and made all the appropriate sounds as they joined the others. Whatever had been bothering them had apparently been tabled.

Jennie closed the sliding glass door. That way she'd hear anyone coming in while she was in Mr. B.'s office. *Quit stalling, McGrady. Let's get this over with.* The office was closed but not locked. She opened the door slowly and slipped inside. Jennie paused to let her eyes adjust to the darkness. Mr. B. had closed his blinds again. Having watched him earlier, Jennie quickly found the chain and carefully opened them a crack. Long strands of light shivered across the desk and up the bookshelf.

Jennie took a deep breath and turned on the computer. In the silence it sounded more like the roar of a jet engine than the purr of an office machine. Once the screen appeared, Jennie pulled up the directory roots and branches and scanned the list. She tried a directory titled "Employee" and found a list of names.

Getting into the directory was easy; finding Rocky's file proved more difficult. There was no listing under Kennedy. Now why didn't that surprise her? On a hunch Jennie tried the r's. Roberts. She accessed the file. Roberts, Edna. Scratch that.

Rochester, Rockford . . . Rockford—Rock—Rocky. Jennie retrieved the file. "Bingo," she murmured. Rockford, Dean; Nickname: Rocky; Age: 20. At least he'd told the truth about that. Male. *No kidding.* Address: 2218 E. 3rd St., Vancouver. She stared at the screen, committing the address to memory.

Shhhh. A soft brushing sound alerted Jennie. The sliding glass door. Someone was coming. *Don't panic, McGrady. It's probably one of the kids.* Jennie tried to concentrate on the computer screen. Just a few more seconds. Click. Jennie's head snapped up at the sound. The door opened.

17

Jennie flipped off the computer and scrambled to her feet. On impulse she grabbed the phone. Watching the door, she raised the receiver to her ear. "Uh-huh. Right. I'm okay, Mom, really." A large figure loomed in the doorway. Jennie swallowed past the huge lump in her throat. "I . . . ah," she stammered into the mouthpiece, hoping Rocky wouldn't hear the dial tone. "I have to go. Talk to you later."

Jennie hung up. *A stroke of genius, McGrady.* She eased away from the desk and moved toward him. "My mother," she explained. "She worries when I'm not home."

"I'd worry too," he said, his eyes piercing like laser beams. "Especially if I had a kid as nosy as you." He stepped into the room and closed the door behind him.

Jennie gave him her best *who me?* look and eased by him. For a moment she thought he'd let her go. As she reached for the doorknob, his arm shot out, blocking her way.

"Don't flash those innocent blues at me, Jennie. I can spot a con a mile away."

Jennie gulped and took a step backward.

"I meant what I said about staying out of this," he

131

went on. "And I don't care if your grandmother is the President. I don't know what you were doing in here, and I'm not going to ask. But don't get me wrong, Jennie. There'd better not be a next time."

He smiled then, catching Jennie off guard. "So, what say we get back to that party where I can keep an eye on you. Since you don't have a date and I'm free, we can finish out the evening together."

Jennie's jaw dropped. Ordinarily she'd have told him to go stick his head in a bee hive. Given her current circumstances, however, she didn't seem to have much choice. One side of her brain reminded her she could go home. The other, as usual, couldn't resist the challenge. *Okay, McGrady, you wanted to know more about Rocky, alias Robert Kennedy, alias Dean Rockford. Here's your chance.*

Rocky held out his hand, palm up. Jennie placed her hand in his. Excitement shivered through her as their eyes met. She quickly looked away. It wasn't the kind of feeling one should have toward a criminal.

———

Except for letting her go upstairs to get into her blue silk dress, Rocky hadn't let her out of his sight all evening. They ate together, talked, and even sang folk and country songs when Jerry played his guitar. Lisa and Allison kept casting furtive glances her way, but she hadn't been able to break away from her bodyguard long enough to talk to them. Even when she'd gone upstairs to change, he'd made sure it was at a time when Lisa and Allison wouldn't be there.

At midnight the band leader announced the last song. "This is a beautiful country song made popular by Garth

Brooks. So everybody sit back and enjoy *The Dance*." Rocky slid an arm around Jennie's shoulders as they sat together at a candlelit table for two. The tables encircled the pool, and a stage had been set up at one end for the band. The stars glistened in the gently rippling water, transfixing Jennie.

"Great song," Rocky said softly.

"Yes. It is." Jennie closed her eyes and let the sweet melody drift through her, imagining herself floating across a dance floor in her rustling blue silk.

She'd learned a lot about Rocky in the last few hours. His favorite singers, colors, and songs. He liked jogging, hiking, swimming, and skiing. He had a sister Jennie's age at home who'd been paralyzed by a drunk driver a few years ago. He had a wonderful laugh and dimples in his cheeks, and when the light hit him just right he looked like one of her favorite singers, Michael Bolton.

Whoa, McGrady. This isn't a date, remember? The guy's four years older than you. Besides that, he could be a stalker. Jennie tried to think of the things she'd learned that might incriminate him. All she had so far was his odd behavior and the fact that he hadn't wanted them to know his name.

When the song ended Jennie straightened and opened her eyes. Rocky's blue ones met hers. He lifted her chin with his fingers, and Jennie wondered what it would be like to kiss him. She wouldn't have minded a kiss. It would have been a perfect way to end the evening.

"Thank you for a great evening," he said softly. His sky blue eyes clouded over. "You're a beautiful girl, Jennie—bright, warm, and alive . . . and I want you to stay that way. You've got to promise me you won't do any more detective work." He took hold of her arms. "Promise me," he demanded. When she didn't answer he tightened his grip.

"Okay," Jennie muttered. "I won't . . . just let me go." Rats, she was going to cry. No way would she give Rocky the satisfaction of seeing that he'd gotten to her. She broke away from him and walked inside.

Fortunately, this was not the throw-yourself-on-the-bed-and-cry-yourself-dry kind of thing. By the time Jennie got to the guest room where she and Lisa were staying, the tears had given way to raw fury. Jennie kicked off her shoes and yanked the bow from her hair. "Ow—" She'd also yanked half her hair off with it.

"Jennie, what's wrong?" Lisa and Allison walked in and barely missed being torpedoed by the silk bow.

"Nothing." Jennie picked up her shoes and stuffed them into her bag.

"When I first saw you and Rocky together," Lisa said, "I thought maybe you were questioning him. Then . . . Jennie, you don't have a crush on him or anything, do you? The way you two were looking at each other to-night . . ."

"No!" Jennie said a little too loudly. "I don't have a crush on anybody. I can't stand the creep." She took a deep breath. "Thanks to you two, he caught me in your dad's office and decided that making himself my date was the best way to keep me out of trouble."

Allison scooped up the bow and dropped into a wicker chair. "Did Rocky . . . I mean, he didn't hurt you, did he?"

Jennie closed her eyes. Hurt. Embarrassed. Humiliated. Used. All of the above. How could she have been so stupid as to think he might have been having a good time . . . that he might have really meant what he'd said about her being pretty? *You let your guard down, Mc-Grady. You let yourself get caught up in music and candle-*

light. You were acting like a girl. Jennie almost choked on that one. She could almost hear Gram saying, "My dear child. Of course you were acting like a girl. You *are* a girl."

"No," she said finally. "He didn't hurt me." To herself she added, *Not physically, anyway.*

"Good." Lisa shrugged out of her dress and shoes and retrieved her sweats. "Did you find out anything?"

"Yeah. According to the file, his real name is Dean Rockford. Lives in Vancouver. I tried to memorize the address. Twenty-two something East Third. I can't remember right now." Jennie unzipped her dress and let it slither to the floor. "It doesn't matter anyway." She jerked on her jeans and a purple University of Washington sweatshirt. "I'm through."

"No!" Allison wailed. "Jennie, you can't give up now."

"Like I told you earlier. Your dad is taking this seriously. He says the police are too."

"Even if that's true," Lisa argued, "the police aren't going to look for another stalker. They have Jerry."

"I'm sorry. Both Rocky and Mr. B. warned me off. I'm not about to go through another night like tonight."

"Listen," Allison said as she rose and headed for the door. "I've got to go back downstairs to say goodbye to everyone. Promise me you'll stay till I get back."

"Look, Allison. I'm tired. I just want to go home and go to bed."

"Please."

Jennie sank onto the bed. "Okay, you win."

Lisa watched Allison go, then closed the door. "Are you really giving up?"

"Forget it, Lisa. It's not going to work." She turned

onto her stomach and buried her head in the soft pillow.

Jennie felt the bed shift as Lisa sat on it. "You want to talk about it?"

"What?"

"You know."

Rocky. The unspoken word hung between them. After a few minutes, Jennie turned onto her back and sat up.

"Lisa, Rocky is arrogant, mean, he uses a phoney name, I'm sure he's involved in something shady, and he could even be the stalker. He could easily have taken Mr. B.'s gun and stashed it in Jerry's pickup. He could have written the message on the mirror, then come down by the pool. He could have followed Allison to my house that night she and B.J. stayed over, and he could have followed me to Crystal Springs. Do you honestly think I could like someone like that?"

Lisa didn't have to say it. The answer was evident in her smile. "He's also cute and very charming." Lisa reached over and gave her cousin a hug. "Oh, Jennie, I love it when you mess up. It makes me feel like there's still hope for me."

At ten minutes after midnight Jennie stopped at a red light and wondered about the wisdom of her decision to drive home alone. Brad—after he, Lisa, and Allison drove Jerry home—would drop Lisa and Allison off at Jennie's. Jennie had already locked the car doors, but she pressed the button again.

Twice she could have sworn someone was following her, but both times they'd turned off. She saw headlights again, about half a block behind her. *Stop it, McGrady. You're being paranoid. If they follow you home just keep going—right to the police station.* Jennie turned off her lights and turned right onto Magnolia Street. She paused just before her driveway and peered into the rearview mirror. Nothing. The car had either turned off or stopped.

Jennie eased the white Mustang into the driveway, wishing she had a color that would blend more easily with the shadows. She found her house key before opening the car door. She'd read somewhere that you could use keys as a weapon by holding the key ring in your hand and arranging them so the keys stuck out between your fingers. Jennie tried it and made a fist. She whistled. "You could poke somebody's eyes out with these."

With her keys still sticking out between her fingers, Jennie unlocked her car door and stepped out. The night had grown cooler. Jennie shivered. The porch light was out. Had Mom forgotten to leave it on? She doubted that. Jennie had called earlier to say she'd be coming. It was probably a burned-out bulb. Or someone had removed it. The stalker wouldn't need to follow her. He knew exactly where she lived. He could be waiting in the bushes right now.

Oh, for Pete's sake, McGrady. Cool your jets. This thing's got you so spooked you're hallucinating.

Squeak—groan. Squeak—groan. The porch swing. Now *that* she hadn't imagined. The wind had come up but not enough to set the swing in motion. Was someone in it? Mom had said she was going to bed. Had she changed her mind?

Jennie slowly climbed the porch steps. "Mom?" she called. No one answered. Squeak—groan. Squeak—groan. . . . Jennie adjusted the keys in her fist. As she reached the top step a shadowy figure rounded the corner.

18

"It's about time you got here." The figure stood between Jennie and the door.

Jennie grabbed her chest to keep her heart from taking off, then clutched the post beside the stairs to steady herself. "You are dead meat," she blurted.

"What?" B.J. leaned against the post on the other side and folded her arms. "Did I do something wrong? I just wanted to stay up to thank you."

"Right. And while you were at it, you figured you'd scare me to death. That wasn't smart." She held up her key-studded fist. "I could have permanently damaged your face."

B.J. took Jennie's hand and lifted it up to where the streetlight offered its faint light. "With this? Ha. That's rich." B.J adjusted the keys. "You got to set them closer to the knuckle so you get a direct hit. Now try it."

"On you?" Jennie tested the keys against her hand. "This is good. Thanks. I'll remember this next time someone tries to sneak up on me."

B.J. ignored Jennie's remark and opened the door. "Come on. Let's go inside. Want some hot chocolate?"

"Sure." Jennie paused at the door and looked up.

"Look, God," she murmured, "I agreed to let her live here, not take over."

Ease up, McGrady, Jennie answered her own objection. *God probably figures you're used to it. Lisa does it all the time.*

Jennie dropped a handful of mini marshmallows in her hot chocolate. "I have to admit, I'm surprised you decided to come. You didn't seem too sociable when I invited you to Jerry's arraignment."

"Yeah, well, I'm sorry about that. I shouldn't have taken it out on you." B.J. stirred her drink, scooped out a spoonful, and blew on it.

Jennie shrugged. "It's no biggie. I'd probably have been pretty teed off too if my folks didn't believe me."

"Hey, McGrady, if that was the problem, you think I'd be here?" B.J. answered Jennie's questioning look with a grin. "Look, I know you think I'm involved in this stalking thing. You just can't figure out where I fit."

"So why did you come?"

"Because you call me B.J."

"Huh?"

B.J. took a sip of her drink. "Look, I admit that it hurts when people don't believe me. But you know what hurts more? When they don't accept me. All I ever hear is Bethany this and Bethany that. I've been B.J. nearly all my life. My *father* says since my given name is Bethany Joy Beaumont, that's what I'll be called. He doesn't like nicknames—he doesn't like me."

"Is that why you call Allison *Al*?"

"Yeah. Doesn't help, though—they still don't get the message."

"I'll admit the name thing is kind of strange, but what about all the stuff they've been doing for you?"

"You mean the clothes?"

"Yeah, and your room. When Allison was showing me around, she told me that she and Mrs. B. had the room decorated just for you."

"For me? Jennie, you saw that room. It's pink. Do I look like a pink person to you? They didn't do that room for me. They did it for the person they want me to be. Mrs. B. insisted on buying me clothes. She didn't once ask what I wanted. Just told me what I needed."

"I'm beginning to see what you mean." Jennie finished off her drink and took their cups to the sink. "So what are you going to do?"

"I don't know. Your mom said I could stay here awhile. I know one thing. . . . I'm not going back until they start calling me B.J."

At ten-thirty on Saturday morning, a busload of weary teenagers and their youth director piled out of the bright blue bus bearing the name *TRINITY CENTER*. Most of the kids had fallen asleep on the way up, probably because of the party at Allison's the night before. At least that was Jennie's excuse.

The motor home in which Mom, Uncle Kevin, Aunt Kate, Nick, and Kurt had traveled was already set up in a beautiful campsite overlooking the river. Jennie stretched and yawned, then went to the rear of the bus to help unload their gear. Tents, backpacks, duffel bags, and food. Mom had assured her they'd packed enough food to feed an army, but as empty as her stomach felt at the moment, she wondered if it would be enough.

B.J. slipped up behind her and pulled out a new forest green backpack and matching sleeping bag. Michael had taken her to a sporting goods store. "What," Jennie had teased when she'd brought it in the house, "not pink?"

That morning Michael had handed Jennie his camera and had asked her to be the official photographer for the retreat. The idea had delighted her. She'd taken a few shots on the bus, which she thought she might use later to blackmail certain people who slept with their mouths open. She pulled the camera out again and snapped some candid shots of the kids setting up camp, then joined them for snacks. Soon most of the kids had drifted off in different directions to explore the area. Since they'd be hiking downriver the next day, Jennie suggested they make the four-mile trek to Middle Falls. Jennie tried to recruit a hiking party but didn't get much response. A few of the guys had brought fishing poles and planned to catch their dinner.

Lisa, sprawled out in a lawn chair, peeked out from under her baseball cap. "I'm saving myself for tomorrow."

"Me too," Allison murmured.

"I'll go," Eddie volunteered. "Where's Paige?"

Mom stuck her head out of the RV. "Lying down. Says she feels nauseated and has a headache. Probably the bus ride up. The fumes and everything."

Mom, Aunt Kate, and Annie, another of Trinity's princesses, elected to stay at the campsite to work on dinner in case the fish idea didn't pan out.

In the end, Jennie headed up the trail with Nick at her side and the camera around her neck. B.J., Michael, Uncle Kevin, Kurt, Jerry, and Eddie followed behind.

Nick had been sticking pretty close to Jennie that morning after he discovered B.J. would be staying at their house. As they walked he kept glancing up at her. The trail snaked along the river, occasionally cutting through the woods. They gained elevation and were soon standing on a precipice high above the river.

Jennie held tightly to Nick's hand as the trail ran along the cliff edge. She had to get a picture and handed Nick off to Michael. "Here, hang on to him a minute. This is going to be a great shot." She stopped to peer over the edge. A shudder ran through her and she quickly stepped back.

"What's wrong, Jennie?" Michael and B.J. asked at the same time.

Jennie shook her head to clear it of the premonition or vision or whatever it had been. "I don't know. I was standing there and all of a sudden I felt myself falling."

"Are you dizzy?" Michael asked as he led Jennie farther away from the edge. "Do you want to go back?"

"No. I'm fine. It's gone now." By the time they reached Middle Falls, they were too tired to go on. Jennie took several photos of the wide, roaring falls as well as the cliffs that rose above them. She was especially pleased with one shot she'd call *Weeping Rocks*. She might not even have noticed if Nick hadn't asked her why the rocks were crying. The kid was a genius.

By the time they got back to camp, the sun had disappeared behind the trees and the air had grown cold. Jennie left the others and walked along the trail to the building that housed showers and bathrooms. Minutes later, as she approached their encampment Jennie spotted a shadowy figure crouched behind the RV. Was it the stalker? Or just a curious camper? Jennie circled around. Then, staying low, she moved from tree to tree hoping to get a better look. She still had Michael's camera. Maybe the telephoto lens would give her a clearer view. Jennie carefully lifted it out of its bag, brought it to her face, and focused. The camera whined. His head snapped up. He stared in Jennie's direction. She lowered the camera and dropped to the ground, listening. The wind whispered through the branches high above her head. Fires snapped, crackled, and popped like amplified bowls of Rice Krispies. She heard the low murmur of voices and occasional outbreaks of laughter. But no footsteps.

Jennie drew in a long, shaky breath and peered through the brush. He was gone. She scrambled to her feet and hurried back into the camp, moving in as close to the fire as she could get. Someone threw another log on. The flames roared up, toasting her skin. As hot as the fire had gotten, it couldn't chase away the lingering chill that seeped into her bones.

The next morning Jennie checked her backpack, going over the list of supplies and emergency equipment Michael had insisted they bring. It was a day-long trip, but they were to be prepared in case they got lost or separated from the group. Extra food, flashlight, matches, and first-aid supplies all packed in a watertight container. Extra clothing in case they got wet. A jacket in case the weather changed. Jennie had no intention of getting separated from the group. Nor did she intend to let Allison out of her sight.

Several times during the night she'd been tempted to tell the others about the figure she'd seen. But what would she say? "Hey, guys, guess what? Someone was sneaking around behind the RV." Yeah, right. In a campground with a hundred people. It could even have been one of their own crowd. Such as B.J., who seemed to enjoy sneaking around in the middle of the night and scaring people. No, Jennie decided, there was no point upsetting anyone. She'd just keep her eyes open—for now.

Only about half the group would make the ten-mile hike downriver. The others would take the bus and RV to Big Creek Falls, wait for the hikers to check in, then head down to their final destination near Curly Creek Falls. Mom and Aunt Kate would take the motor home, two very unhappy boys, and a still very sick Paige with them. Chad Bishop, Annie's boyfriend, volunteered to drive the bus and promised to bring all the leftover gear.

At seven a.m., after breakfast and a sunrise service, Michael, acting like a cross between a boy scout leader and an army sergeant, gave everyone a final check and moved them out. Jennie crouched down one more time to say goodbye to Nick, who was heartbroken because he was not allowed to go on the big hike. He'd wrapped his arms around her neck so tightly Jennie thought she'd need a wrench to pull him off.

"But I wanted to go with you," he pouted.

"I know, but you can't walk that far. You'll have a lot more fun with Mom. Kurt has to stay too."

"Jennie," Michael barked. "Get the lead out. We're leaving—now!"

Jennie gave a sarcastic salute and muttered, "Yes, sir." Aloud she yelled, "I'm coming!" By this time she'd disengaged herself from Nick, the group had disappeared from view, and Jennie ran to catch up. A lone hiker walked the trail ahead of her. His muscular brown legs, worn boots and pack told Jennie he must be a veteran on the trails. "Excuse me," Jennie said as she overtook him.

"I'd pace myself if I were you, Jennie."

Jennie spun around to face him. She knew the voice all too well. "What are you doing here?"

144

19

"My job." Rocky grinned and shifted his pack.

"Watching Allison?" Jennie asked.

"And you." He winked. "Tough job, but someone has to do it."

"Last night, behind the RV. That was you, wasn't it?"

He raised an eyebrow and shook his head. His expression softened. "Ah, Jennie. What am I going to do with you?"

The warmth and wistfulness in his eyes turned Jennie's brain to mush.

"Come on," he added, dropping an arm around her shoulders and drawing her forward. "We'd better not let them get too far ahead."

When she brushed against him, Jennie felt the familiar shape of a shoulder holster. The kind her father used to wear. Rocky was carrying a gun. The realization startled her, but she wasn't frightened by it. When it came to Rocky, especially after Friday night, her senses seemed to have taken a vacation. He could be the stalker, and here she was walking with him. Alone. In the woods. Common sense told Jennie to run. Yet, being with him made her feel strangely secure.

"Jennie." Michael appeared on the trail ahead of them. "You're okay. When you didn't catch up I got worried." He glanced from Jennie to Rocky then back again. "I see you've met Mr. Rockford." He extended a hand to Rocky. "Thanks for looking after her."

Jennie stared at the two men as the profile on Dean Rockford, alias Rocky, alias Robert Kennedy, began to take shape in her head. *Oh, McGrady, you are such a klutz. You should have known.* The phoney name, pretending to be a gardener and all-around handyman. She should have seen it the first time she'd met him—the way he'd questioned her about the flowers, and the warnings he'd given her to stay off the case. They weren't the sinister threats of a stalker. "You're a cop."

Rocky raised an eyebrow. "Undercover. Beaumont hired me to protect Allison and investigate the case during my off hours. If you really want to help, Jennie, I'd suggest you join the others and pretend we never had this conversation."

———

Relieved to have her questions about Rocky answered and knowing he was with them gave Jennie an opportunity to relax. The scenery along the river was spectacular. The trail snaked through giant firs, cedars, and mossy undergrowth. She stopped frequently to take snapshots of wild flowers, the river, and the group. At one point on the trail Michael shushed them and pointed through the forest to a doe and her two fawns. With the telephoto lens Jennie got several close-ups. Ryan would be sorry he missed it.

Six miles and a couple dozen photos later, they reached the falls area where they were to rendezvous with

Mom, Aunt Kate, and the other non-hikers. Jennie's legs felt like rubber. They still had about four miles to go before they reached the Curly Creek area, and she hoped the brief rest and lunch would revive her.

Michael and Uncle Kevin had dropped back to prod Allison and Lisa along. Jerry, Ed, and Brad had reached the falls and had crossed the river on a fallen log by the time Jennie and B.J. arrived. "Is this the only way across?" Jennie asked, peering at the wildly churning river as it rolled under the log, then dumped itself over a fifty-foot cliff only a couple of yards beyond her. "I've seen balance beams wider than that log. You sure it's not rotten?" Somehow she'd imagined they'd cross over on a nice sturdy bridge—with sides.

Ed, Jerry, and Brad, complaining that they were near starvation, disappeared along the trail that led to the parking area.

"I don't know," Jennie said to B.J. above the roar of the falls. "I think we should wait for the others."

"You can wait. I'm going across." B.J. stepped onto the log and darted across as if she'd done it a hundred times before. She slipped on the last step but managed to make it onto the mossy bank.

"Come on across, McGrady," B.J. called. "It's a piece of cake."

Jennie took a deep breath and stepped onto the log. She tried not to look at the water rushing beneath her. *You can do it, McGrady. Just concentrate on putting one foot in front of the other.* She took two more steps, wobbled slightly, and put her arms out for balance. "Jennie, don't!" Michael yelled from the riverbank. "It's too . . ."

Crack! The log exploded under her. Jennie plunged into the icy water. She struggled for a foothold and clawed at the rocks and roots as the river dragged her along. Her head popped out of the water. Jennie took a deep breath. The river sucked her under again and she felt herself going over the edge.

You're going to die, McGrady. Instinctively, she tucked her body into a ball to lessen the impact. *Falling, falling.* Her shoulder hit bottom first, then her leg. *This is it.* Jennie waited for the inevitable. Any minute she'd float away and an angel would greet her and take her to heaven.

Jennie needed air. What was going on? She'd gone over the falls with thousands of gallons of water. Been dashed against the rocks. Had she already died? Was God just going to leave her there? Or banish her to . . . Wait a minute. She was still holding her breath. Her lungs ached and she was ready to explode. That meant she had to be alive. *You won't be for long, McGrady.* She couldn't hold her breath much longer. Her maximum time was about two minutes.

Her shoulder brushed against something solid and flat. Jennie reached for it, but the water pulled her away. Something sharp scraped at her leg. Jennie grabbed at it and connected. As she followed the ledge her head surfaced. Jennie hauled in as much of the moist air as her lungs would hold, then using her handhold for a step, hoisted herself farther out of the water.

It was dark and damp. She'd surfaced in a cave behind the falls. The icy mountain water had turned the cave into a refrigerator. She shivered. The river had eaten her alive. Her fingers tingled from numbness. Her head ached. From somewhere in the depths of her memory bank, Jennie dredged up the word, *hypothermia.* A condition where the body temperature drops to dangerously low levels. Jennie couldn't remember how long it took. Fifteen minutes, maybe twenty.

She let her backpack slip from her shoulders, unhooked the belt around her waist, and hauled the pack around in front of her. After managing to undo the ties, Jennie dragged out her soggy clothes, then reached for the airtight container. She bet Michael hadn't had this kind of emergency in mind when he'd made the kit mandatory gear.

Jennie fumbled with the flashlight. Her fingers, numbed by the cold, refused to work, so she pushed the switch forward with her teeth. The beam bounced off steep jagged walls. Water thundered from the precipice high above her head and spilled into a deep pool. With the volume and force of water, she'd never make it to the other side of the falls. She'd been lucky the first time. No way would she try it again.

"Don't get me wrong, God," she murmured. "I'm thankful to be alive, but you gotta help me find a way out of here." Jennie shuddered. "And soon." The cold had penetrated through to her bones and Jennie had begun to shiver uncontrollably. A massive curtain of water enclosed the cavern. To her left, the rushing water hugged the rocks, making it impossible to pass. To her right, the falls curved around and disappeared behind a rock wall. Jennie inched forward. Letting her body slide back into the icy water, she followed the rock wall around the corner to get a better look. At the far right of the falls, a jagged outcropping of rock penetrated the massive waterfall. Water careened off both sides of the boulder, but for a space of about two feet, occasional splotches of light splintered the darkness.

Jennie had no way of knowing what lay on the other side, but she had to try it. With her left arm looped through the straps of her backpack, she headed for the opening. The turbulent water along the rocky edge was only a few feet deep. Within a few minutes she splashed through the falls to the sunlit world on the other side. Jennie stumbled, trying to stay erect as the river pushed her along and finally dumped her on the shore. Dragging her pack out of the water, Jennie collapsed on the narrow bank.

You made it, McGrady. Jennie closed her eyes. It wouldn't be long now. *They'll see me and . . .* Jennie's mind switched into slow motion, *everything . . . will . . . be . . . all right.*

When she awoke, rocks pressed against her face and arms. Something the size of a boulder jabbed at her side. As she tried to move, pain coursed through her shoulder. She groaned. "What. . . ?"

Jennie opened her eyes, shading them from the blinding sun. How long had she been lying there? Her mouth felt dry and hot. Her clothes were warm but still damp. Jennie reached for her canteen, untwisted the top and took a long drink, then splashed some on her face.

Why hadn't anyone come? She glanced around, trying to get her bearings. She was lying downstream of the falls, maybe about fifteen feet away. Solid rock walls, brush, and trees lined the river for as far as she could see. The trail they'd come in on was high above her. Why wasn't anyone there? They wouldn't just leave her. Unless . . . "Oh . . . God, they think I'm dead. They think my body was washed downstream."

Stop it, McGrady. This is no time to get hysterical. Just stay calm. There's got to be a way out. She called for help.

A crow answered with a sharp caw that sounded like a cruel laugh.

Jennie pulled her knees up and tried to stand. A sharp pain ripped through her leg. A long blood-caked gash ran along her calf from just above her sock to her knee. The cut blurred as tears stung her eyes. *Come on, McGrady. Don't give up now.* Jennie drew in a long, shuddering breath and wiped an arm across her face.

Obeying a strong, steady voice in her head, Jennie grabbed the metal frame of her pack and crawled into the shade of a tree that stood beside the river. Its roots curved around the rocks and reached into the water like tentacles. She splashed cool water on her face and arms, then poured some on the wound. After washing most of the dried blood away, Jennie retrieved the first-aid kit. She rummaged through assorted bandages and finally settled on a roll of white gauze.

When she'd finished wrapping her leg, she leaned back and rested her head on the soggy clothes she'd taken out of her pack. Her head still hurt. She felt so tired. Jennie closed her eyes and drifted into a long dark tunnel.

———

"Jennie!" Michael's voice drifted through the darkness, bringing her back. "Can you hear me?" A loud fluttering noise nearly drowned him out. She opened her eyes. Michael and Uncle Kevin were kneeling beside her. A helicopter hovered above their heads. "Hang on, kid." Michael smiled down at her. "We'll get you out of here."

"Mom . . ." Jennie tried to lift her head.

"Don't try to move," Uncle Kevin warned. "We don't know if anything is broken. Your mom is up there." He

151

pointed to the helicopter, where a stretcher was being lowered down.

"W-what happened?" Jennie murmured, as bits and pieces of the fall filtered back into her mind.

"Just relax, Jennie," Michael crooned. "We'll talk about it later."

———

The fact that Jennie had survived the accident, the doctor told her, had been a miracle. The only injuries she'd sustained had been the gash on her leg, a mild concussion, and a badly bruised left shoulder. "Everything else looks okay," he'd said. "But I want to keep you overnight—just in case. Your body took quite a beating, and I want to make certain we didn't miss anything."

Mom and Michael were the first visitors allowed in to see her. Mom brushed the hair from Jennie's forehead and stroked her brow, then leaned over the rail and kissed her.

"Jennie," Michael began, "I can't tell you how sorry I am. I thought there would be a way across the river. A guy at school told me . . ." He shook his head and looked away. "I should have checked it out."

"It wasn't your fault," Jennie assured. "I shouldn't have tried to go across. It held the others so I thought it would hold me too. Guess I'm going to have to go on a diet." When they didn't respond, Jennie sighed. "Hey, lighten up, you guys. I survived."

"No thanks to that crazy hunter," Michael muttered.

"Hunter?" Jennie glanced from Michael to Mom and back again. "What hunter?"

Mom looked totally disgusted. "Michael, you promised. I didn't . . . Never mind."

"Susan, I'm sorry."

Mom ducked out from under his arm and turned toward the door. "I have to check on Nick."

Michael watched her go. He pulled his fingers through his thick sandy-brown hair. His hazel eyes looked tired and sad. "I don't seem to be racking up very many points with your mother lately."

His deep sigh tore at Jennie's heart. *What's the matter with you, McGrady? You've been praying for Mom and Michael to break up. You should be thrilled they're having problems.* "She'll get over it," Jennie heard herself say.

"I hope so." He glanced toward the door again. "I love her, Jennie. I don't know what I'd do if things didn't work out for us."

Jennie didn't know what she'd do if they did. "So," she said, changing the subject, "what weren't you supposed to tell me about this hunter?"

Michael explained that her fall had been caused by a stray bullet. Rocky had stayed behind to investigate. Someone had shot through the bark. "It's no wonder you fell. A shot like that would be like having a firecracker explode under you. The ranger said they'd been having trouble with poachers in the area and figure some hunter missed his target and hit the log. Unfortunately, you were on it at the time."

20

Over the next couple of hours while Mom kept a steady vigil at her bedside, visitors streamed in and out. Kevin, Kate, Lisa, Brad, Paige, Ed, and most of the other kids who'd been on the hiking trip. *But not B.J., Allison, or Jerry.* Jennie couldn't help but wonder why.

That night when the visiting stopped, and she'd finally persuaded Michael and Mom to go home, Jennie chewed over the details of the fall like a dog with a bone. Michael had said the shot had probably been fired by a hunter. A stray bullet. A coincidence? Maybe, but Jennie couldn't help thinking about the other possibility. What if the stalker had carried out his threat against her? What if he was closing in on Allison and wanted her out of the way?

Jennie dug into her memory for details or clues that would reveal the shooter. Ed, Jerry, Brad, and B.J. had all crossed before her. Could one of them have collected a gun and come back? She immediately dismissed Brad, then added him back on as a possible suspect. He was Lisa's boyfriend, but how much did she really know about him?

B.J. couldn't have fired the shot. She had been waiting on the other bank when Jennie fell. And from what Lisa had said the night before, B.J. had practically drowned trying to save her. Still, Jennie couldn't help wondering why B.J. hadn't come to see her in the hospital. The theory that she might be working with someone surfaced again.

What about Ed? He'd been going with Allison, they'd broken up, and now he and Paige were engaged. But something was definitely wrong with that picture. Jennie remembered the strained look on their faces the night of the party. Now that Jennie thought about it, the shooter could have been Paige. She hadn't gone on the hike. Had Paige feigned illness, then waited in the woods to ambush her? It would be easy enough to check it out. Tomorrow she'd ask Mom.

Even though Jennie resisted the idea, the most logical suspect was Jerry. She had no idea whether Brad, Ed, or Paige could handle guns, but as much as she hated the thought, Jennie couldn't help remembering Jerry's knowledge and expertise with firearms. Had he hidden one in his pack? Had he slipped away from the others to keep her off the case for good? But why? He had Allison now. She adored him. Jennie shuddered as she remembered reading a suspense novel where this guy dated girls, then killed them because they reminded him of a girl who thought she was too good for him.

Jennie shook her head. That was too bizarre. She'd known Jerry for years. Still . . .

Jennie drifted in and out of sleep as the nurses checked her vital signs and shined a flashlight in her eyes to check her pupils and ask her stupid questions like: "What's your name?" "Do you know where you are?"

"Standard procedure for head injuries," they told her.

When she awoke early the next morning, the scent of flowers permeated the air. Jennie stretched and glanced over at the shelf along the wall that held the cards, carnations, roses, and plants her family and friends had brought. She reached for the water glass on her nightstand and nearly dropped it.

Sometime during the night someone had added a long-stemmed, wilted black rose to her collection of flowers. Jennie gasped and held back the urge to scream. A card beside it in block print read, *Sorry you made it. Next time you won't be so lucky.* It took a moment for Jennie to grasp the cryptic meaning. Then it hit her. The questions she'd been brooding over during the night—the hunter had been after her and had been in her room last night.

Jennie fought back the rising wave of hysteria. With trembling hands, she reached for the phone to call the police. The door of her room swooshed open.

Rocky stepped in, closed the door behind him, and leaned against it. His long blond hair drooped around his shoulders, framing his unshaven face. His haunted expression echoed his words. "She's gone."

"Allison?" A chill swept through her like an Arctic wind. "What happened?"

Rocky dragged a chair up to the bed and folded himself into it. "After you fell, I stayed behind—thought maybe I could track down the shooter. Figured she'd be okay returning on the bus with the youth group. I hadn't counted on Rhodes letting the Shepherd kid drive her home from the church."

"What do you mean?" Jennie felt like she'd been doused with ice water. "You don't think Jerry . . ."

"Jennie, I know he's your friend, but you have to face facts. The guy carries a rifle in his truck—he's won awards for marksmanship. He and Allison haven't been seen since they drove out of the church parking lot last night.

156

I figure he shot at you to distract us. It worked. After what happened to you, I—"

"Jerry wouldn't shoot me." Her argument sounded weak, but having a person like Jerry betray her—no, she couldn't accept that. "You told Michael it was a hunter."

"I didn't want to worry them until I had some facts to back up my suspicions." He drew both hands through his hair, then leaned forward and rested his arms on the bed. His troubled blue gaze moved up to meet hers. "It wasn't an accident, Jennie."

Jennie swallowed and looked toward the rose. "I know. I just didn't want to admit it. That was here when I woke up."

Rocky studied the note. "Did you call the police?"

"I was just about to when you came in."

Rocky grabbed the phone and punched out the numbers.

Two hours later, the police had come and gone. No prints, no clue as to who might have entered the hospital with a dying black rose.

The doctor had released Jennie, and Rocky insisted on driving her home. When they reached the house, he took a look around, then escorted her inside. "After what happened to Allison, I'm not taking any chances. From the looks of that note, Shepherd might come after you next. I'm sticking to you like glue."

The thought of Rocky hanging around for what could be days unnerved her. "Is that really necessary? Nothing's going to happen to me here."

"Trust me, it's necessary."

"But what about the Beaumonts? Shouldn't you be trying to find Allison?"

"Donovan and Mendoza are handling that. Besides,

Beaumont's fuming—doesn't want me near the place. Dragged Rhodes and me over the coals so many times we've got first-degree burns on our backsides."

"He's upset with Michael?"

"Let's see, how'd he put it? 'If anything happens to my daughter, neither of you will ever work in this town again.' Yeah. I'd say he's upset."

After talking with Mom and touring the house, Rocky took up residence in the living room. B.J., who'd been watching a soap, muttered a few unintelligible words and stomped upstairs.

"B.J. has been like that ever since yesterday afternoon." Mom came up behind Jennie and gave her a hug. "With you falling and then Allison disappearing—I know she's really upset, but she won't talk about it. Just keeps it all inside. I wish there were something we could do for her."

"Maybe I could talk to her," Jennie said.

"I'm so glad you're home." Mom hugged her again and handed Jennie a package. "I almost forgot. This came for you Saturday—I think. And Lisa called. Said it was urgent. Oh, and Paige wanted you to call her as soon as possible." Mom frowned. "I'm worried about that girl. I told her she should see a doctor, but she said she already had. Let me know how she's doing when you talk to her, okay?"

"Sure. Oh, Mom, where was Paige yesterday when I did my daring-fall-over-the-falls trick?"

"That's not funny. I don't know how you can joke about it."

"Sorry . . . umm . . . what about Paige?"

"She didn't leave the trailer until we heard you'd fallen. Why?"

"Oh, nothing," Jennie said as she glanced at the envelope Mom had given her. "I was just curious."

Jennie practically ran upstairs. She would call Paige and Lisa later. The package in her hand, with a return address that read *Debbie Cole, Dolphin Island, Florida* demanded her immediate attention. Jennie hurried to her room and tore it open. Inside she found several photos and a note from Debbie.

Just wanted to tell you how much we enjoyed your visit. I was going through an old photo album from my college days and came across these pictures of your dad. Thought you might like to have them. If you're ever in Florida come see us.

Debbie

P.S. Sarah says she and Samson miss you, and Scott wants to know if you're ready for another game of pool.

Jennie smiled. The image of Scott with his protest signs drifted into her mind. "I wish I could," she said wistfully.

"Wish you could what?"

Jennie's heart bounced all over her chest. She spun in the direction of the voice. "You scared me half to death. I didn't know you were in here."

"Join the crowd. No one else does either." B.J. stepped out of the window seat and set a book she'd been reading on the cushion. "A letter from your boyfriend?"

"No, a friend." Jennie told her about Dolphin Island, Debbie and Ken Cole, Sarah and Scott.

"Sounds like a neat place. Are these pictures of Scott?" B.J. asked.

Jennie clutched the photos to her chest.

B.J. frowned and flopped back onto the window seat. "Forget I asked."

Nice going, McGrady. "I'm sorry." Jennie perched on

159

the seat beside B.J. "They're of my dad when he was in college. You can look at them with me if you want."

With B.J. looking on, Jennie leafed through the photos of Dad in his college years. When they'd finished she returned them to the envelope, then carefully tucked them into her journal, promising herself she'd get back to them later when she could study them alone.

"Think they'll find Al?" B.J. asked.

Jennie dropped onto her bed. "I don't know."

B.J. climbed out of the window seat and rearranged the pillows and stuffed animals. "I'm thinking of going over to see my dad and stepmom," B.J. announced.

"Really?"

"Yeah, but don't pack up my stuff just yet. I'll probably be back."

"What made you decide to go?"

"Just some things Michael said about family. He said, 'You never realize how important they are to you until you lose them.' "

"Michael said that?"

B.J. nodded. "Told me he lost his wife and six-year-old boy about ten years ago in a car accident. I didn't think I liked Al much. We didn't have anything in common. Now that she's gone . . ." B.J. picked up a stuffed lop-eared bunny and caressed the ear. "I kind of miss her. Anyway, I'm going."

"What about your name and the pink room?"

"Like I said. I may be back."

Since Mom was busy with Nick, Jennie talked Rocky into taking B.J. home, assuring him that she'd keep the doors locked. After they'd gone, she went in search of

Mom and Nick and found them asleep in his bed under a dozen or so books. She went back to her room to examine the photos from Debbie.

She'd just pulled out her journal when the phone rang. "Jennie, where have you been? Why didn't you call me back? I told your mom it was urgent."

"You say that all the time," Jennie protested. "How am I supposed to know when you really mean it?"

"I always mean it. Anyway this *is* urgent. Paige called me. She said she left a message for you too. Did you call her?"

"No. I—"

"Well, never mind. She's picking me up and then we'll swing by to get you."

"I can't go anywhere." Jennie tucked her journal back into the drawer and closed it. Jennie told her about the dead rose she'd found in the hospital room that morning.

"That's awful. I can see why you'd be worried, but you can't stay cooped up in the house forever. Besides, you wouldn't be going out alone. Paige and I will be with you. Look, Jen, I wouldn't ask you to go, but Paige is really upset."

"Can't it wait? I promised Rocky."

"I don't think it can. She's pregnant . . . and she's threatening to kill herself."

21

Jennie scribbled off a quick note to Mom and Rocky to tell them she was going out for a while with Lisa and Paige. She'd just returned to the living room when a gray car pulled up in front. Jennie jumped back from the window. *Easy, McGrady,* she told herself as Lisa emerged and waved. *You're jumpier than a frog with fleas.*

Jennie drew in a ragged breath. Seeing the gray car, even if it wasn't *the* gray car, reminded Jennie that the case was far from being solved. Someone driving a gray car had pulled a gun on her and Lisa—and had followed Jennie into the Crystal Springs Gardens. *Okay, McGrady. The stalker did have a gray car. But this is Paige. She's pregnant, for Pete's sake—and suicidal.*

Jennie hurried down the walk and crawled into the backseat behind Paige. She leaned up and squeezed Paige's shoulder in greeting. Two round spots of color on Paige's cheeks tried to disguise her pale skin, and failed miserably. "Umm . . . would you like me to drive?" Jennie offered. "I mean, if you're not feeling well . . ."

"N-no, I'm fine." Paige glanced at Lisa. "Did you tell her?"

Lisa nodded.

"It's just morning sickness." Paige lifted a trembling hand to the gearshift.

"Are you sure?" Jennie asked again, reluctant to ride with someone her cousin had described as suicidal.

"M-maybe you're right," Paige said. "It would be better if you drove."

Jennie and Paige switched places. After familiarizing herself with the vehicle, Jennie put it into drive and pulled away from the curve. "Nice car," she said, admiring the plush gray leather seats and wishing Mom could trade their '85 Buick in for a newer model.

"It belongs to my parents. They've gone out of town for a few weeks. Don't worry," she answered Jennie's unspoken question. "I have permission to use it."

"Where are we going?" Jennie asked.

"Just head for the Sunset Freeway."

"I thought you wanted to go to Clackamas Town Center." Lisa sent Jennie a worried look.

"I don't want to be around a lot of people. I hope you don't mind." Her already soft voice had become even softer.

"It's okay with me." Jennie eased the car onto the freeway.

Paige leaned forward in her seat. "Isn't it awful about Allison's kidnapping?"

"Kidnapping?" Jennie asked.

"You didn't know?" Paige became more animated. "I called this morning to see if they'd heard anything about Allison. They got a call from the kidnapper demanding a $500,000 ransom."

The hairs on Jennie's arms stood on end like tiny antennae that had just picked up some important message. Why hadn't Rocky told her?

"Do they still think Jerry did it?" Lisa asked.

"They're not sure what to think." Paige leaned back in her seat. "The caller was a woman."

They drove in silence for a few minutes. Jennie glanced back at Paige, who'd gone white again and looked as though she were going to be sick.

Paige pointed ahead and to the right. "Pull off at the next exit. I need to make a phone call."

They found a pay phone near the first gas station. Jennie stepped out of the car to stretch her legs while Paige slipped into the phone booth and Lisa went into the food mart for drinks. She watched as Paige dialed a number. She must have gotten an answering machine because she spoke continuously for about thirty seconds, then hung up. A smug look of satisfaction crossed over her face. It was fleeting, but unmistakable. *Something strange is going on here, McGrady. Paige might be nauseated and nervous, but she's no more suicidal than you are.*

When Lisa arrived with drinks, Jennie jogged over to the passenger side and opened the door for her. As she went back around the car she glanced at the license plate and stopped dead. The last two numbers were zeros. The same as those on the car in the Murrays' driveway.

Jennie tried to visualize Paige as the stalker, but couldn't. The person who'd held a gun on her and Lisa and who'd called that night had been taller, and Jennie felt certain it was a man. Or at least it had sounded like a man. *It could have been Ed.* The thought lodged itself in her mind.

Paige opened the door of the phone booth and walked toward her. She had that worried look again. *Your imagination is running away with you, McGrady. Paige is pregnant. She and Ed are engaged. Their parents are rich—they certainly don't need the money*. Besides, Jennie rationalized, the stalker's gray car had a cellular phone. This one didn't.

"Jennie," Paige came up beside her. "Are you coming? Is something wrong?"

Jennie drew in a deep breath. "No, I'm fine. I was just trying to decide whether or not I wanted some corn chips."

"I'd rather you didn't. My folks don't like me to eat in their car. Anyway, the smell of those things makes me sick."

Jennie slid under the steering wheel, trying to decide what to do next. Was this the car? She needed to be sure. Jennie glanced at Paige in the rearview mirror. "Too bad you don't have a cellular phone," Jennie said. "You could have called while we were driving."

Paige's gaze met Jennie's. "We do. Only Dad took it with him."

Jennie tried not to let the impact of Paige's revelation show in her face. She concentrated on snapping on her seat belt, adjusting the mirror, and putting the key in the ignition. A hundred questions tumbled through her mind. Why had Paige lied to get Lisa and her out here? Was Ed in on this too? Or someone else? What could she do about it? Somehow she had to let the police know.

"What are you waiting for?" Paige sounded irritated. "Let's go."

"Um . . . I think I'll use the rest room while I'm here."

"I don't think so." Paige leaned forward. Jennie felt something cool and hard press into the back of her neck.

"J-Jennie," Lisa squeaked. "Sh-she's got a gun!"

"Don't get any ideas, Jennie. I do know how to use it. Now start driving."

For a moment Jennie's mind went blank. She gripped the steering wheel, desperately fighting off the urge to scream. *Stay calm, McGrady. Stay calm. You can do this. God, please help me.* Jennie twisted the key in the ignition and the motor roared to life. She took a deep breath and let it out slowly, put the car in drive, and drove out of the parking lot.

Paige directed her back toward the freeway and told her to head for Cannon Beach. "Where are we going?" Jennie asked.

"Up to the cabin."

"Cabin?" Lisa and Jennie asked at the same time.

"Yeah. My folks have a cabin only an hour from here. It's in the coast range, on the Elk River—not very far from Cannon Beach. You'll like it there." She frowned, then smiled. "I don't know why I said that. You won't be able to go to the beach—at least not for a while."

Jennie eased onto the freeway heading west. "Is that where you're hiding Allison and Jerry?"

"Just shut up and drive." Paige's sharp response and the way she shoved the gun deeper into her neck told Jennie she'd guessed right.

Don't panic, she told herself. *Stay calm and try to keep her talking.* "Look Paige, we're on a freeway here. Do you think you could take the gun out of my neck—it's getting really hard to concentrate on driving." Jennie was surprised at the strength in her voice. "I'd hate for us to get killed in a car accident."

Paige pulled the gun back and positioned herself behind Lisa. "All right. But try anything and Lisa dies."

Good move. She cast Lisa a look that said *I'm sorry.* Lisa, eyes big as tennis balls, gripped the armrest and shot back a look of barely controlled panic.

166

Obviously Lisa wasn't used to this. Jennie almost laughed at the thought. *And you are? Okay, McGrady. Enough. She's got you, and there's nothing you can do for now except play along.* Or was there? She may not be able to escape at the moment, but she could ask questions.

"Why are you doing this, Paige? I never pegged you as the criminal type."

"I'm not a criminal." Paige sounded genuinely surprised.

"Last time I looked, kidnapping was a federal offense. So is threatening a person at gunpoint. Which reminds me. Was it you or Ed that shot at me up at the falls?"

"He didn't shoot at you—he shot at the log. We just wanted to scare you. It wasn't his fault you went over the falls."

"What about the kidnapping? Was that an accident too?"

"I didn't mean . . . just shut up, Jennie. I'm not going to talk about it anymore."

"Okay, just one more question, Paige. Are you really pregnant, or was that just a trick to get Lisa and me to come with you?"

"I-I'm pregnant."

"How does Ed feel about it?" Jennie asked.

"At first he wanted me to get an abortion, but I told him no way. He's gotten used to the idea. He wants us to go away and start a new life together . . . " Paige's voice trailed off.

Jennie was beginning to get the picture. Ed had instigated the whole thing. He'd promised Paige a marriage and a home. Somehow she couldn't picture Ed as a devoted husband and father. Paige was holding on to a fairy tale and was willing to do anything to make it come true.

Apparently Lisa had gotten the same message. The fear in her eyes had subsided. She turned in her seat and looked back at Paige. "You really love Ed, don't you?"

Paige swallowed and blinked back the tears forming in her eyes. "He loves me too."

Now why didn't you think of that, McGrady. You were trying to get to her brain. Lisa is getting to her heart.

"You must have been really happy when Allison broke up with him," Jennie said.

Paige stiffened. "She didn't. Eddie dumped her. He said Allison lied to him about me. She'd told him I didn't like him anymore."

"That's terrible," Lisa empathized. "You must have been furious with her."

Paige nodded. Anger contorted her face, erasing any beauty that had been there. "We both were. We decided she needed to be taught a lesson. When I found out she was getting flowers from Jerry . . ."

"You knew it was Jerry all along?" Jennie interrupted.

"Yeah. He told Eddie what he was going to do."

"So you sent the dead flowers and made threatening phone calls to scare her." Jennie's patience was wearing thin. "You figured the police would suspect Jerry of those too. How could you do something like that?"

Lisa cleared her throat. "Don't mind Jennie. She doesn't understand what it's like to really be in love with someone." When Paige didn't answer, Lisa continued. "It must be scary being pregnant and getting married."

"You know what would scare me?" Jennie glanced back at Paige. "I'd be afraid Ed would run off with the money and leave me to face charges of kidnapping."

"Eddie wouldn't do that!" Paige shouted.

"I bet he's got the ransom money and is buying a ticket to Mexico right now."

"Well, you're wrong. He's meeting me at the cabin. When we've gotten away we'll call the police and tell them where you are."

"I don't think he'll show up. And even if he did, he'd find a way to get rid of you. Ed's not about to settle down . . ."

"Shut up!" Paige screamed. "I know what you're doing. You're trying to turn me against him. Well, it won't work."

Maybe not now, but the seed is planted. Jennie tucked the knowledge away. As she drove in silence, Jennie mentally kicked herself. Why hadn't she seen it before? She'd suspected Paige and Ed, but only briefly. It didn't make sense to stalk and kidnap someone over a few dates. Jennie couldn't imagine anyone being so vindictive. She tried to imagine how she'd feel if Ryan dumped her for another girl. She'd be upset, hurt, but she couldn't see herself being angry enough to commit a crime.

Paige and Ed had to be stupid—or desperate to go this far. *And you weren't too bright either, McGrady. You should have known the minute you saw her gray car pull up. You shouldn't have gone.* Jennie silenced the accusing voices. It wouldn't help to keep bemoaning the fact that she'd messed up. As Gram would say, "There's no use kicking a dead horse." It was too late to change the past. All she could do now was look for a way out. Maybe at the cabin. Jennie felt certain Allison and Jerry would already be there, and maybe between the four of them they could stop Ed and Paige.

———

Forty minutes later, Paige motioned them off the main road and onto a narrow, winding driveway. Serenity Lane, the sign read. Jennie almost laughed at the irony of it. Jennie felt about as serene as a thunderstorm.

The cabin sat in a cleared area at the end of the drive. "Looks like Ed's not here," Jennie said as she stepped out of the car.

"He will be." With the gun still trained on Lisa, Paige motioned them inside. The cabin had a damp, woodsy smell. Smoothly finished logs lined the interior. A stone fireplace covered one wall, and across from it, an open stairway led to a loft.

"Nice house," Jennie said absently, dropping back so she could slip between Lisa and Paige. If she could distract Paige somehow, maybe she could knock the gun out of her hand.

Jennie looked up at the loft. "Is that where you're hiding Allison and Jerry?"

Paige glanced up for an instant. Jennie slammed a fist down on Paige's wrist and sent the gun skidding across the floor. She grabbed Paige's forearm, spun her around, and held it taut behind her back.

"Ow, let me go!"

"Lisa, get the gun."

Lisa didn't move. Her gaze was fixed at the top of the stairs. "I-I d-don't think that would be a very good idea, Jennie," Lisa stammered.

"Smart girl." Ed leaned over the railing, a gun casually hanging from his hand. He raised his arm and pointed it at Jennie. "Let her go."

22

Jennie dropped Paige's arm and the girl stumbled forward, retrieved the gun, and glanced up at Ed. "I didn't think you were here. Your car . . ."

"I left it in Portland and hitched a ride with a trucker. Police are probably going crazy by now." Ed laughed and waved his gun, then settled his sights on Jennie again. "Glad you two could come. Jerry, Allison, and me were having this really interesting conversation. Jerry thinks I should let them go, give the money back, and tell everyone I'm sorry. I told him I'd think about it on my way to California."

"You're not going to get away with this," Jennie said.

"Of course we are." He pulled some cord out of his back pocket and tossed it to Paige. "Tie them up."

"I can understand kidnapping Allison," Jennie said as Paige drew her hands behind her back. "But why us?"

"You're the detective. You figure it out," Ed barked.

Jennie didn't even try. He was obviously worried that sooner or later she and Lisa would realize that he was the gunman at the Murrays' that night. As Paige wound the rope around her wrists, Jennie balled up her fists and strained against the rope, hoping there'd be enough slack to work them loose later.

When Paige finished tying Lisa, Ed directed Allison and Jerry downstairs. Jerry had a black eye and swollen lip, but the way he jerked away from Ed's hand told Jennie he still had some fight in him. Maybe there was some hope after all. Allison, however, wouldn't be much help. Ed half carried her down the steps. Her drooped and matted hair partly covered red-rimmed eyes and a bruised cheek. She whimpered as he dumped her on the floor at the bottom of the stairs. Allison didn't look much like a princess anymore.

The thought infuriated Jennie. B.J. had called him "pond scum." Jennie had a few choice descriptions of her own. She wouldn't voice them though, not now. She couldn't risk him getting mad at her.

While Paige held her gun, Ed looped a rope through the ties on their ankles and secured Jennie, Lisa, and Allison to the post at the bottom of the stairs. As soon as he turned his back, Jennie started working at the knots on her wrists, hoping to loosen them more.

He ordered Paige to wait in the car, then put a gun to Jerry's back and shoved him out the door. "Jerry, my man. It's time for us to take a little ride. But first . . ." Ed opened the door and led Jerry out to the porch.

Donning a pair of garden gloves, Ed picked up a can of kerosine and sprinkled fuel all over the front door and porch. He grabbed one of Jerry's hands and pressed it to the can, then heaved the can into the front yard.

Jennie stared at him for a moment. Then the realization of what he was planning seeped into her brain. He was framing Jerry. The police would find Jerry somewhere, no doubt with a ton of evidence to tie him to the kidnapping and the cabin containing the charred bodies of three girls.

Paige tore up the porch steps and grabbed Ed's arm. "What are you doing? You can't burn . . ."

Ed threw her off. She stumbled backwards and fell against the porch railing.

"What's the matter with you? I told you to get in the car."

Paige scrambled to her feet. "No, you promised no one would get hurt. You said . . ."

"Shut up. Either get in the car or get in the house with them. One more body isn't going to make that much difference."

There was enough slack in the ropes to where Jennie had been able to work her hands free. Now all she had to do was undo those around her feet without Ed noticing. Jennie eased her hands forward and began untying the knots. She glanced up just as Paige looked inside.

You're dead, McGrady.

Paige hesitated, her brown eyes filled with indecision. *Don't tell him,* Jennie pleaded silently. *Please.*

Paige turned back to Ed. "I'm sorry," she breathed. "You know I hate to see anybody hurt. But if you think it's necessary." Paige clung to his arm and kissed his cheek. "Of course I want to go with you."

Jennie let out the breath she'd been holding. She didn't know what Paige had in mind, but she'd be ready.

"That's better," Ed said. "Now put him in the back seat and get in the car."

Paige lifted the gun and pointed it at Jerry. "Move."

"Good girl." Ed pulled a lighter out of his pocket and flicked it.

At that moment Jennie scrambled to the door and dove for his legs. A gunshot ripped through the air and Jennie heard a thud as it reached its mark.

173

Tears stung her eyes as she rolled away from Ed. She felt the rise and fall of her stomach as she sucked in air and slowly let it go. Paige knelt beside him, cradling his head, her fingers dripping with blood from the gunshot wound to his head. Her gun lay on the ground a few feet away where she'd dropped it. "I'm sorry, Eddie," she sobbed. "I just couldn't let you hurt them. It wouldn't have been right."

Running on adrenalin, Jennie brushed away her own tears and got to her feet. She untied Jerry and he hurried in to release the others and to call 911.

In the bathroom, Jennie found a towel, which she took outside and pressed to Ed's wound. "Hold it tight," Jennie instructed Paige, doubtful that their efforts would do much good. She put an ear to his chest, but only heard the distant wail of sirens.

Moments later a squad car pulled in to Serenity Lane. Donovan, Mendoza, and Rocky spilled out with weapons drawn. Somewhere deep down Jennie knew they'd come. She just wished it hadn't taken them so long.

Later that evening, when their statements had been taken and everyone had gone home, Jennie tried not to think about the broken girl Donovan and Rocky had arrested. Or about the boy who lay in intensive care, hovering between life and death. She tried not to blame herself. Tried not to tell herself that if she hadn't tackled Ed, Paige might have hit his leg or shoulder instead of his head.

Instead she concentrated on the positive things—the fact that Donovan and Mendoza had put a tracking device in the suitcase holding the ransom money. And Rocky, after finding her note, tracked down Paige's parents, found out about the car and the exact location of the cabin.

Michael, who'd stayed at the hospital with Ed's parents, called to tell her that Ed had undergone surgery and was in "stable but critical condition."

Allison and Jerry had been released from the hospital earlier. Their bruises would heal quickly—at least those on the outside. The police had dropped the charges against Jerry, and tomorrow they were all going to meet at Allison's to debrief and go swimming in the pool.

B.J. had whittled the chip on her shoulder down to the size of a small house. She'd decided to stay with the Beamonts that night. "Allison might need me," B.J. had said. "You know how fragile she is."

Jennie glanced at the figure sleeping in her window seat and smiled. It had taken Lisa an hour to persuade Aunt Kate and Uncle Kevin to let her spend the night. She breathed another prayer of thanks that they were all alive and not buried in the smoldering remains of an isolated cabin.

All these things, the bad and the good, Jennie entered in her journal as a letter to her dad. Almost as an afterthought, she wrote:

I made a new friend who's a rookie cop. Not a boyfriend—more like a big brother. You'd like him. His name is Rocky. Really it's Dean Rockford. He wants me to meet his sister, Pam. Maybe I'll invite them to Allison's pool party tomorrow.

Then again, maybe not. He'd probably lecture her again on following orders.

As Jennie closed the journal, she pulled out the envelope she'd placed in it earlier that day. Once more, she looked at the pictures of her father. Jennie smiled back at the young Jason McGrady with the dark blue eyes and wide, carefree grin. Debbie had written the dates on them and Jennie figured he'd only been about nineteen at the time. When she got to the last picture, she paused.

The man with his arm looped around Ken and Debbie bore little resemblance to the young man in the other photos. He was older and wore a dark heavy beard. She turned the photo over. On the back Debbie had only written the names *Jason, Debbie, and Ken—Fort Meyers Beach, 7/7/88.* She looked at the picture again.

"This can't be real," she whispered. A huge lump formed in her throat, making it almost impossible to breathe. The picture had been taken two months after her father had disappeared.

Jennie hugged it to her chest. She wanted to wake everyone in the house—to shout the good news to the world—especially to her mom. *Dad is alive! See, I told you* . . . But a voice inside cautioned her to keep silent.

"Okay," she whispered. "At least until Gram comes home." Jennie tucked the pictures back in her journal, stashed it in her nightstand drawer, and turned off the light.